S0-BAS-513

"I'm looking forward to working with you, Miss…?"

The woman's cheeks turned a pretty shade of pink. She tucked a strand of her wavy hair behind one ear. "Oh, I'm sorry. My name is Nichelle Latimer."

She grasped his hand. Her fingers were small and delicate and sent an awareness like a sudden sugar rush through his system.

"My family owns this store."

Questions popped into his mind. Why wasn't her family here helping? She must have sensed his curiosity because she tugged her hand away.

"Which way to the stockroom?"

She pointed toward the back. Ethan nodded and attempted a smile, but he couldn't quite manage it. Sometimes he thought he'd forgotten how to smile.

He turned and walked toward the rear of the building. Nichelle. It was a lovely name for a lovely woman. But the guarded look in her eyes suggested she was protecting herself from something.

The lady had secrets.

But then, so did he.

Books by Lorraine Beatty

Love Inspired

Rekindled Romance
Restoring His Heart
Protecting the Widow's Heart
His Small-Town Family

*Home to Dover

LORRAINE BEATTY

was born and raised in Columbus, Ohio, but has been blessed to be able to live in Germany, Connecticut and Baton Rouge. She now calls Mississippi home. She and her husband, Joe, have two sons and six grand-children. Lorraine started writing in junior high and has written for trade books, newspapers and company newsletters. She is a member of RWA and ACFW and is a charter member and past president of Magnolia State Romance Writers. In her spare time she likes to work in her garden, travel and spend time with her family.

His Small-Town Family

Lorraine Beatty

HARLEQUIN® LOVE INSPIRED®

If you purchased this book without a cover you should be aware
that this book is stolen property. It was reported as "unsold and
destroyed" to the publisher, and neither the author nor the
publisher has received any payment for this "stripped book."

Recycling programs
for this product may
not exist in your area.

LOVE INSPIRED BOOKS

ISBN-13: 978-0-373-87924-3

His Small-Town Family

Copyright © 2014 by Lorraine Beatty

All rights reserved. Except for use in any review, the reproduction
or utilization of this work in whole or in part in any form by any
electronic, mechanical or other means, now known or hereinafter
invented, including xerography, photocopying and recording, or in
any information storage or retrieval system, is forbidden without
the written permission of the editorial office, Love Inspired Books,
233 Broadway, New York, NY 10279 U.S.A.

This is a work of fiction. Names, characters, places and incidents are
either the product of the author's imagination or are used fictitiously, and
any resemblance to actual persons, living or dead, business establishments,
events or locales is entirely coincidental.

This edition published by arrangement with Love Inspired Books.

® and TM are trademarks of Love Inspired Books, used under license.
Trademarks indicated with ® are registered in the United States Patent
and Trademark Office, the Canadian Intellectual Property Office and in
other countries.

www.Harlequin.com

Printed in U.S.A.

Trust in the Lord with all your heart
and lean not on your own understanding;
in all your ways submit to Him,
and He will make your paths straight.
—*Proverbs* 3:5–6

To my brother Ken Carswell. I miss you every day.

Acknowledgment

A special thank-you to Dr. Ronda Wells
for her medical help with Sadie's fever.

Chapter One

"Nicki, how long do you think you can keep this up? Running the store, taking care of a new baby, then going home at night to help your parents. You're wearing yourself out."

Nichelle Latimer could feel the disapproving eyes of her friend Debi Gordon on her back as she straightened the display of spiral notebooks in her family's office-supply store. They'd been friends since junior high, and Nicki knew the concern was sincere. Just not welcome at the moment.

"I don't have a choice. I'm the only one who can help right now. Mom has to focus on Dad's recovery. He's doing well after his kidney transplant. He doesn't need to worry about the store."

But Nicki was very worried. Since coming home to Dover, Mississippi, six months ago, she had willingly stepped in to help run Latimer's Office Supply. The work had kept her busy and focused on something other than the death of her husband and the legal and emotional trauma he'd left behind. It hadn't taken long to realize that business was slow and customers few and far between. But it wasn't until she'd returned to work after having her daughter, Sadie, and assumed management of the store that she'd realized the extent of the problem. If something didn't change soon, Latimer's Office Supply would be out of business.

The old brass bell over the door jingled, announcing the arrival of a much-needed customer. Nicki gave her friend a quick hug. "Don't worry. I'll be fine."

Debi gave her a skeptical frown before turning to leave. "Call me if you need me."

Nicki dealt with the customer, then reached for her cell phone to check on Sadie. She missed her so much. It was the first time she'd let her mother babysit, and that was only because she needed time alone to examine the store's accounting files.

As she did, her heart sank. If she didn't find a way to increase business soon, her parents would be ruined. They were counting on her. What she needed was a full-time employee, someone she could depend on. She'd placed a Help Wanted sign in the front window three days ago, but no one had even inquired. Strange, considering the bad economy. Surely someone needed a job. As soon as the store was closed, she'd draft an ad for the *Dover Dispatch*.

An hour later, the bell over the front door of Latimer's jingled again. Nicki glanced at the clock in her small office in the back of the building. There was still an entire afternoon to get through before she could close up and go home to Sadie. Weariness threatened to drag her down. She closed her eyes and sent up a prayer for strength. Not that God would hear her feeble plea. He'd stopped listening to her years ago when she'd turned her back on Him and stepped into a nightmare.

Walking out onto the sales floor, she put on a smile for the incoming customer. Her gaze landed on a tall, dark-haired man standing inside the door. She didn't recognize him. In a town the size of Dover, strangers stood out, and this man wasn't likely to be overlooked. With his broad shoulders, the dark stubble shadowing his angular face and his piercing dark eyes, he looked hard—dangerous, even. His dark chocolate hair lay in appealingly tousled waves, making his deep-set, black-coffee eyes even more noticeable. Those eyes narrowed slightly. He'd noticed her staring. She forced her gaze from his and to the object he held in his hand. Her Help Wanted sign.

"May I help you?"

The man smiled. Sort of. One corner of his mouth moved, which brought a faint light into his eyes. A small scar below his left cheek added intrigue.

He held up the sign. "Is the position still available?"

"Yes, it is. Are you interested?"

He handed her the sign. "Possibly. I'd like to know a little about the job." His intense gaze skimmed her length before looking her in the eyes again.

A rush of warmth filled her cheeks when she saw a glint of appreciation in his brown eyes. Mentally, she shook herself for such a ridiculous thought. She must be more tired than she realized. She swallowed and cleared her throat. "Stock work, to begin with. I'm going to be reworking the entire layout of the store, so there will also be a lot of physical labor."

A quick inventory of his well-developed chest, the muscles straining the sleeves of his shirt and the strong thighs encased in faded jeans confirmed he was more than capable of moving the displays. The man had slipped his hands into his front pockets, with his head slightly tilted, his dark eyes narrowed. She realized with a jolt that she was assessing him as he had her earlier. "Um, then if it works out, I'll need someone to work the sales floor."

The man nodded. "Sounds good."

"Are you looking for full time or part time, Mr....?"

"Stone. Ethan Stone. Either, but full time would be preferred." The corner of his mouth moved again, distracting her and revealing a deep crease in his cheek and tiny crinkles at the corners of his eyes.

"Do you have any retail experience?"

"I paid my way through school working at a big-box store. I did time in nearly every department."

A man who worked his way through school showed determination, but something about him didn't seem right. While he looked scruffy and hard, his words and his posture were that of an educated man. Not some down-on-his-luck drifter looking for a minimum-wage job. Too many years with her deceitful late husband raised her defenses. Why would an educated man want a job as a stock boy? She crossed her arms over her chest. "I have a feeling you're seriously overqualified for the job, Mr. Stone."

He raised his eyebrows, his dark eyes questioning. "Can anyone be overqualified for honest work?"

The glint she'd seen in his eyes was now a full-blown twinkle. Was he baiting her or manipulating her? She raised her chin. "You're not from around here."

"No, ma'am. I got into town yesterday afternoon."

His deep voice rolled along her nerves. "Where are you from?"

He shrugged and lifted the corner of his mouth a bit more. "Here and there."

"Where have you worked before?"

"Several places. Mainly out of the country."

He wasn't giving her much incentive to hire him. She

opened her mouth to tell him she didn't think he would be a good fit for the job, but before she could speak, he took a step forward. She tensed, then relaxed when she saw his eyes soften, and the crooked grin lifted on the other side.

"If you need a reference, you can call Jim Barrett."

"Pastor Jim at Peace Community Church? You know him?" This changed everything. Jim wouldn't recommend any old vagrant.

Stone nodded, pulling his hands from his pockets and resting them on his lean hips. "I'm good friends with his brother Paul. We…worked together."

"Oh. I see." She tried to find a reason to turn him down, but she was desperate and needed someone who could start immediately. The doorbell sounded again as several customers entered, triggering the urgency that gnawed in her chest every hour. She couldn't leave Dover until the store was in the black, and if she was going to save the store, she had to have help. "How soon can you start?"

He glanced over his shoulder as the door chimed again. "Now."

Moving behind the checkout counter, she pulled a sheet of paper from the shelf, then lifted a pen from the small container beside the register and handed both items to him across the counter. "Fill out this application, please. You can sit at one of the desks over there. When you're finished, we'll discuss your hours and pay."

"Will do." With a nod, he turned and strode toward the display of office furniture in the far corner of the sales floor.

Nicki watched him with an uneasy sensation in her chest. He walked like a man confident in his abilities.

A man who could handle himself in any situation. A soldier, perhaps. But even that idea didn't fit. He didn't have the high-and-tight haircut or the ramrod posture she'd seen in her marine brother. Something was off. She just couldn't figure out what it was.

Remembering she had customers in the store, she shoved the thoughts aside. She was being overly sensitive. She couldn't paint every man she met with the same brush as her late husband, Brad. Just because a man was reserved and private didn't mean he had something to hide.

She glanced at the man again. Despite her misgivings, there was something trustworthy about him. History had taught her to be cautious, but she had to start trusting her instincts again. *Please, Lord, let this be the right decision, because I'll need his help and Yours to save the store.*

Ethan wrote his name on the line, trying to remember the last time he'd filled out an employment application. He'd worked for TNZ News Network since graduating college. But that job had ended ten months ago. His years embedded with the troops as a conflict photographer had resulted in capturing one too many horrific images with his camera. The doctors had called it cumulative stress disorder. He called it an emotional meltdown.

Ethan blinked away the visions lurking in the back of his mind and wrote down Jim Barrett's name as a reference. Jim's brother Paul had been the lifeline Ethan needed after he'd returned from his last assignment in Afghanistan. He'd been wounded and emotionally traumatized, and the military shrinks hadn't been able to help him much. But then he'd returned to Atlanta, met Paul and joined his post-traumatic stress disorder group for civilians. Not only had the group turned his life around, but Paul had become a close and valued friend. When Ethan had been looking for a place to start his life over, Paul had sung the praises of his small hometown in south central Mississippi.

He was giving himself two months to see if Dover could be his new home. Having a job would help him settle in. Within a few minutes he'd filled in all the blanks with his scant personal information. He hoped she wouldn't press him for the background facts he'd left out. He carried the paper back to the front, waiting while the woman completed a sale to a customer.

She smiled and took the application from his hand. His heart did a funny little twitch inside his chest. She was a very attractive woman with her shoulder-length blond hair and eyes the color of cornflowers in summer. He guessed her to be a few years younger than himself. The top of her head was even with his shoulder, and it was hard to ignore her nice curves. There was a softness about her that intrigued him and reminded him of the delicate pink azaleas in bloom all over town.

She glanced at him, and he saw a wariness in her blue eyes. Not that he could blame her. He didn't inspire confidence with his two-day growth of beard and old faded shirt. He'd deliberately chosen to keep his appearance low-key, hoping to blend in and not call attention to himself. Had he realized the Lord would lead him to Latimer's Office Supply, and a job interview, he'd have done things differently.

The woman took a moment to look over his application. He braced himself for the question she would undoubtedly ask—the one that asked for an emergency contact. The one he normally put his previous boss's name in. Not this time. He had no intention of letting Karen Holt know his whereabouts. She'd want him to come back to work. Out of the question. His life as a conflict photographer was over. As long as he stayed away from his camera, he should be okay. He had absolutely no intention of looking through that viewfinder again.

The bell over the door jingled again, preventing her question. She glanced briefly between him and the new customers. He saw the doubt in her blue eyes fade and knew she'd decided to take him on.

"Why don't you take a few minutes to look around the store, familiarize yourself with the merchandise? We'll talk as soon as I take care of these customers." She shoved his application into a drawer behind the counter and started to walk off. "Oh, I'll need someone who'll stay on the job for several weeks. Is that going to be a problem?"

The determined lift to her chin belied the hopeful look in her blue eyes. His protective instincts stirred. The lady could use a hand, and helping others had been one of the things that restored his sense of purpose. "No, ma'am. I'll stay as long as you need me."

Ethan took a quick tour of the store while the woman waited on a customer. The first thing that struck him was the size of the place. It was too large for one person to manage alone. Which might explain her desperate need to hire the first person who walked in the door.

He made his way through the store, walking down aisles set in neat predictable rows and gazing at the merchandise one would expect in an office-supply store. The back corner held an assortment of office furniture. The area next to it displayed a small selection of outdated computers and printers. One thing was evident. Latimer's Office Supply was a basics-only store. In fact, it bordered on old-fashioned. But maybe that was the norm for a small Mississippi town.

Overall, it was a charming business. He dragged his hand along his jaw. Nothing here would trigger a memory. Nothing here would yank him back to the past. It was the perfect place to start over. No memories would be stirred. No old nightmares resurrected. He'd promised himself he'd learn to be a participant in life and not merely an observer.

Returning to the sales counter, he found the woman— he didn't know her name yet—staring at the departing customer. "Where would you like me to start?" Her gaze collided with his, the blue eyes wide and filled again with a shadow of doubt.

She smiled and raised her chin slightly. "The stockroom. But first we need to discuss your hours and pay."

Ethan started to tell her he wasn't concerned about wages, but she stated an amount before he could speak. "Sounds fair."

"Good. For now, you'll have Sundays off, but I'll be making a lot of changes, and I'd like you to come in on Mondays, too. At regular pay."

"That'll work."

"Good. I've lost several employees, and I need to replace them quickly."

"Understood." He extended his hand. "I'm looking forward to working with you, Miss…?"

The woman's cheeks turned a pretty shade of pink. She tucked a strand of her wavy hair behind one ear. "Oh, I'm sorry. My name is Nichelle Latimer."

She grasped his hand. Her fingers were small and delicate and fluttered against his palm, sending a sweet jolt of awareness like a sudden sugar rush throughout his system.

"My family owns this store."

Questions erupted in his mind. Why wasn't her family here helping? She must have sensed his curiosity because she tugged her hand away and squared her shoulders.

"Which way to the stockroom?"

She pointed toward the back. Ethan nodded and attempted a smile, but all he could manage was a nod. Sometimes he thought he'd forgotten how to smile. He turned and walked toward the rear of the building. Nichelle. It was a lovely name for a lovely woman. But the guarded look in her eyes suggested she was protecting herself from something. The lady had secrets. But then, so did he.

The back hall was positioned on the east side of the building and led directly to the back door. On the right was an office, and tucked between it and the rear entrance was a kitchen and eating area. The stockroom was on the opposite side and extended along the back wall of the building. Boxes and packages were stacked on the floor and piled on the worktable, waiting to be opened.

The familiar surroundings eased the slight tension from his shoulders. The stockroom was a good place to start. He was comfortable here. He could do his job with little interference. One thing his new boss had mentioned made him uneasy. Waiting on customers. Dealing with people face-to-face had never been his strong suit. It was why he'd lived his life behind a camera lens. No chance for emotional entanglements that way. But he was jumping the gun. There would be time to worry about that later.

Ethan reached for the box cutter on the shelf and slit the seam of the closest carton. Spiral notebooks. It was spring. School would be out soon. Maybe Nicki was planning ahead for back-to-school sales. Prying off the packing slip, he verified it against the contents, then moved on to the next box. He glanced at the assortment of pricing tools hanging above the worktable. He'd have to speak with his new boss about price points for the merchandise.

His lips moved into a smile. The activity reminded him of his college years working at the discount store. The Lord had come through for him again. There was absolutely nothing in Latimer's Office Supply that would remind him of the Middle East or suicide bombers or innocent victims in marketplaces.

Nicki winced at the sound of the heavy pot being set down on the counter. Her mother was not happy. The nice, quiet Saturday evening meal with her parents had ended in an argument. Nicki had avoided telling her mom about Ethan as long as she could. But when she asked her straight-out when she planned on replacing Charlie, their longtime employee who had recently retired, Nicki had had no choice but to come clean.

"You hired a stranger to work in our store? Some vagrant off the street?"

"Myra, calm down, dear. Nichelle has good instincts about people."

Good thing her father knew how to handle her mother because she surely didn't. They had never been able to communicate. Her brother, Kyle, had been her mother's favorite, always able to charm her out of a bad mood with a wink and a smile. The perfect child who could do no wrong in her mother's eyes.

Opening the packet of formula, Nicki poured it into the baby bottle, attached the cap and shook it. Hard. Kyle *had* been special. She'd adored her older brother and missed him terribly. His death in Afghanistan two years ago had left a huge hole in all their lives. Especially her father's.

"Allen, she hired a full-time employee, some stranger to work our store. He could rob us blind. Or worse."

A twinge of concern inched its way up Nicki's spine. Her mother wasn't wrong. She *had* hired a stranger. But her father was right; she did have good instincts about people. Except when she married them. Then she was a complete idiot. She'd fallen for Brad's charm and his wealth, blithely ignoring the little twinges of doubt until it was too late. But her impression of Ethan was different. She had some questions about him, but she just knew he wasn't a crook.

"Mom, I called Jim Barrett and he vouched for Ethan."

Her mother huffed and shook her head. "I don't like this."

Nicki exchanged glances with her father. "Mom, I need help at the store. I can't run it alone. You have to take care of Dad, and he's got weeks of recovery ahead. What would you like me to do?"

Her mother turned to glare at her. "What do you know about this man?"

"He's experienced in retail and he can work the hours I gave him. That's all I need to know right now." She'd been impressed with Ethan. He'd worked diligently, caught on quickly and only approached her a couple of times with questions regarding the pricing of the merchandise. He looked her in the eyes when he spoke and left the stockroom neat and tidy at the end of the day.

"For all you know, he could be the one robbing the stores downtown."

Allen Latimer peered over his glasses at his wife, a sure sign he was becoming irritated. "Myra, let the girl do her job. She has her hands full with our granddaughter and our business. Don't make things worse."

"Fine. But if one thing is missing from our inventory..." She turned back to the sink, her shoulders stiff with displeasure.

Nicki moved to the baby bouncer on the counter and unbuckled her fussy daughter's safety strap. She took the little girl into her arms, cradling her close and kissing her cheek, reveling in the new-baby smell. She gave Sadie her bottle, smiling at the sweet little sounds she made as she ate, gently bouncing her as she walked into her parents' living room and settled down in the rocker.

She looked forward to this time of day, holding Sadie in her arms as she ate, talking to her, sharing her big plans for their future. From the moment the nurse had placed Sadie in her arms, she'd realized she'd found what she'd been looking for all her life. Something that gave her purpose and happiness—being a mom.

The only thing missing was her independence. She'd planned on striking out on her own once Sadie was born, but that plan had been complicated by her father's kidney transplant and a mountain of red tape with Brad's estate. As soon as she took care of things here, she'd find a job and leave Dover behind.

Nicki glanced up when her dad stood beside the rocker. He gently stroked Sadie's little head.

"She's beautiful. Like her momma."

Her daddy had always been her biggest cheerleader. She didn't like keeping things from him, but after realizing the dire financial situation Latimer's was in, she'd called her friend Gary Palmer to go over the books for her. She hadn't told her father what she'd done for fear of upsetting him. She didn't want to risk a setback. Still, her concern warred with her conscience. What if keeping her dad in the dark only upset him more?

"Dad, about the business…"

Her dad patted her shoulder. "I know. Business has fallen off since Office Mart opened over in Sawyer's Bend. But I've made arrangements to transfer some funds to get things back on track. I meant to do it sooner, but then the transplant donor was found, and I never followed up. You do what you think is best for the store. But let's keep this between you and me. I don't want to upset your mother." He rubbed his forehead. "You know, pumpkin, we're happy to have you back home, and that little darling is our treasure, but I never planned for you to have to take over the store. I'm only sorry this health thing of mine has messed up everything."

Nicki's heart ached. "Oh, Daddy, you haven't messed anything up. I'm glad I was here to help. Besides, I like having something to do every day." For too many years, she'd been denied that choice.

Her father eyed her closely. She could never deceive him. He always knew when she was keeping things hidden, and right now she was hiding a lot.

"Nicki, honey, why did you come home so suddenly, and why didn't you bother to attend your own husband's funeral?"

Shame and guilt washed over her. She focused her gaze on Sadie, who had nearly emptied her bottle. How could she explain the past two years to her parents? They would never understand. Her mother thought Brad had hung the moon. Wealthy, charming, handsome and successful. Everything she'd hoped for her daughter. How could she tell her that Brad had turned out to be a white-collar criminal, that he'd died in a plane crash while attempting to flee the country? And how did she explain that she was broke because Brad's assets were tied up in a federal investigation?

Her dad touched her cheek gently. "When you're ready to talk, we'll be here."

All she could do was nod. She could barely come to terms with how she—an intelligent, educated woman—had been so foolish and gullible. She'd lost herself in her relationship with her husband. Now she had to figure out who she was and who she wanted to be.

Chapter Two

Ethan shook the hand of Reverend Stoddard, uttered a few polite phrases and stepped outside into the Sunday morning sunshine. Two different sermons today had provided plenty of spiritual strengthening. He'd attended Peace Community's early service, eager to hear Jim Barrett preach. Then after a quick cup of coffee and a sweet roll at the Magnolia Café, he'd crossed the park and attended the late service at Hope Chapel. He'd enjoyed both services, but if he was going to join the PTSD group that Jim had referred him to here, he needed to support the church. That meant attending Hope Chapel on a regular basis.

As he took the steps down to the sidewalk, someone called his name. He looked around to see a giant of a man coming toward him, hand outstretched and a friendly smile on his face.

"You're Ethan Stone, aren't you? I'm Ron Morrison. Jim Barrett told me about you."

He nodded and shook the man's hand. Ethan stood an inch over six feet, but Ron's bulk made him feel short. Ron ran the only PTSD support group in Dover. "How did you know who I was?"

"Jim Barrett gave me a good description. Besides, I know the look."

Ethan smiled ruefully. "Yeah, I guess you do."

Ron gestured toward the sidewalk. "Why don't we go over here and talk, if you have the time?"

Ethan fell into step beside him until he stopped at a dark blue Silverado parked at the curb near the end of the block.

Ron pulled a business card from his jacket pocket and handed it to Ethan. "We meet every Wednesday night in a room off the church gym. It's not a large group. We average around five men, sometimes up to eight or ten. There's no pressure to talk or share. You do that when you're ready, or not at all. I just wanted you to know you're welcome, and we're here if you need us."

The card had Ron's number and the church's office number. He'd made a lot of progress in the past ten months. The flashbacks were under control, even though they still lurked in the dark edges of his mind, and it had been months since he'd had a nightmare. But he also knew ongoing support was vital. Paul had taught him to take it one step at a time. Face one fear at a time. He planned on following his friend's advice. "Thanks. I appreciate that."

Ron shook his hand. "We're all in this together. Don't forget that."

Ethan crossed over into the lush park surrounding the courthouse, his gaze taking in the charming nineteenth-century town. Dover, Mississippi, was exactly as Paul had described. From the town square with its majestic courthouse, bandstand and giant live-oak trees, to the charming brick buildings lined up on each side.

April in Mississippi was a riot of color. Pink, red and white azalea bushes and colorful vines exploded from every corner. His photographer's eye automatically began composing the perfect angles to capture the spring display. But he didn't have a camera anymore and he wouldn't ever again. He'd spent his entire life with the lens between himself and the real world. No longer.

"Afternoon, sir." A soldier dressed in camouflage fatigues strolled passed, nodding a greeting.

Every muscle in Ethan's body tensed. Caught off guard, the steel gate holding back his memories shook violently, allowing pieces of the darkness to slip through the cracks. He fought to maintain emotional control and keep his anxiety at bay.

The Lord is my shepherd. The twenty-third psalm had been his anchor during recovery. Slowly the emotional storm in his chest eased, and he started back down the sidewalk.

It had all happened too quick. One minute he had been taking pictures of the soldiers on patrol and locals at the neighborhood market, his lens focused on a mother and infant who had stepped into the frame. The next, fire and debris had rocked him off his feet. He'd continued shooting, keeping the lens to his eye, but the image that emerged shredded his soul. The mother and infant who had been standing near the market were lying on the ground.

Something in his soul had died in that moment.

The next thing he remembered was waking up in a hospital with shrapnel in his arm, a concussion and his emotions churning inside his gut like a tornado. Ten months later, here he was, still trying to get past what he'd seen, vowing to never take another photograph again.

After stopping at Filler-Up-Burgers, a charming old gas-station-turned-restaurant, Ethan returned to his small room at the Dixiana Motor Lodge on the edge of town. The old-style motel was right out of a 1940s postcard. Small cabins laid out in an L shape were connected by a common roof and separated by narrow openings for parking a car. The interior provided all the modern conveniences, though the decor was a throwback to another era. After only a few days, however, the room was starting to close in on him. He'd have to find an apartment or a house to rent now that he'd gotten a job and was committed to remaining in Dover. Maybe he'd ask his new boss for some suggestions.

He was looking forward to work tomorrow. Working at Latimer's would give him a purpose and cover the service part of his rehabilitation. Ron's group would provide the talking. Both were important keys to managing his PTSD. The service part he embraced. The talking, not so much. But as much as he hated to admit it, talking did help. With the Lord's help, he'd learn to open up more, letting go of the fears one memory at a time until the past no longer had a stranglehold on his mind.

Paul's advice had been spot-on. Dover was the perfect place to find himself, to start fresh. Nothing here would drag him down into the darkness. He knew without a doubt that the Lord had brought him here to begin again.

All he wanted now was someplace quiet and peaceful to make a fresh start. He wanted roots. Permanence. He'd lost himself on a dusty street in Afghanistan, and he'd come to Dover to find out who he was now and where he would go from here.

"Good morning."

The deep baritone with the husky rasp sent an unwelcome tingle along Nicki's nerves. She didn't want to notice Ethan Stone. Not as a man, anyhow. Only as an employee. A much-needed and efficient employee. One who arrived on time on a Monday morning, ready to work.

"Hi." She glanced up to find him standing on the threshold of her office, that lopsided smile softening his chiseled features. It would be easier to think of him as someone who worked for her if he weren't so handsome. So capable and so disturbing. Thankfully he was a man of few words who went about his job with efficiency and determination.

He looked more intriguing today. The stubble did little to hide the strong square jaw and high cheekbones below those beautiful brown eyes. He wore an unbuttoned red cotton shirt over a white T-shirt and dark jeans that hugged his legs. He was the image of strength and dependability, two things she needed right now.

She'd learned the hard way not to depend on anyone but herself. She'd teach her daughter that lesson early. The only thing she needed to depend on now was that Ethan would hang around long enough to help her get the new layout in place. She was holding out hope that Gary's findings wouldn't drastically alter her plan to remodel Latimer's.

"Would you like me working back in the stockroom today?"

For some reason, she had a hard time seeing Ethan working in a stockroom, even though he'd worked there all afternoon on Saturday. He looked more suited to the outdoors. She could easily see him leading a safari or heading up some archaeological dig or maybe even exploring jungles. She brushed the fanciful thoughts aside. "Uh. No, actually, I have some sales I need to set and fixtures I want moved."

He nodded. "Point the way."

Nicki stood and came around her desk. She'd anticipated Ethan stepping back out of the doorway to let her through. Instead he stepped farther into the office. They collided in the doorway, wedged together. Nicki found herself with her hands pressed against his chest and with Ethan's hands grasping her upper arms. She refused to meet his gaze, but she couldn't ignore the warmth under her palms or the solid mass of his chest as it rose and fell beneath her hands. She held her breath, forcing herself to focus.

"Uh, the display window." She pushed past him into the hall, taking with her the lingering scent of soap and musky aftershave. She made a mental note to keep a safe distance from Ethan Stone.

"First, I want to dismantle this window display. Then these smaller shelves down here need to be taken apart and stored. You can put the merchandise in the back for now. I want two gateleg tables placed end to end right here. You'll find them in the stockroom near the furnace."

Ethan stood beside her listening intently, hands resting on his lean hips. "Having a sale?"

"Yes. A 'Get a Jump on School' sale. All this old merchandise has got to go." She turned to find his lopsided grin in place. Like before, it warmed his dark eyes, but this time she was close enough to read the glint of appreciation in his gaze. For her? Silly thought. She took a step back only to snag her jeans on the corner of one of the old aluminum shelves. She tilted backward. Ethan's strong hand clamped on to her arm. She grabbed his other arm to steady herself, acutely aware of the muscles beneath her hand. Quickly, she let go and straightened.

What was wrong with her today? When had she become such a klutz? "See why I want these things out of here?"

"I'll take care of it."

Moving to the wooden checkout counter positioned deep inside the store on the east wall, she tapped it lightly. "I'd like to move this counter closer to the front door."

Ethan hunkered down, tapped the wood, examined the base, then stood and did the same on the other side. "I think it's only screwed down. It shouldn't be too hard to move it. It'll leave some ugly scars on the floorboards though."

"Can you do that? Move it, I mean?"

"Yes. But are you sure you want to?" He stood brushing dust off his hands. "Putting it closer to the door might create a congestion problem on busy days. The customers coming in are going to be forced to move around the ones in line."

He was right. Nicki'd been thinking only of the aesthetics, not the practicality. Her poor judgment at work again. She bit her bottom lip. "I'll think about it. Let's leave it for now."

After Nicki pointed out a few more changes she wanted to do quickly, Ethan went back to the stockroom, and she went to check on Sadie. After her talk with her mother the other night, Nicki had harbored some doubts about hiring Ethan without properly vetting him. Her confidence in her ability to make good decisions was fragile, and her mother's comments had stirred her insecurities like the blades of a blender. Now Nicki knew she'd made the right choice. Ethan was capable, handy and willing to follow her direction.

Nicki tiptoed into the small room off the office, which she'd transformed into a mini nursery, to check on Sadie and found her sleeping soundly. She never tired of watching her little daughter. Gently, she stroked her downy soft hair, listening to her sweet baby breaths. Her heart swelled with a love so strong tears threatened to burst forth. How was it possible to love one small person this much?

Back at her desk, she checked on the store bank account. Her dad had followed through. The account balance now showed a healthy total. There was enough to pay the outstanding bills and make most of the changes she wanted to do. Of course, it all hinged on what Gary found in the books.

Movement drew her attention to the doorway as Ethan walked past, carrying a bulky gateleg table in each hand. He carried them as if they were nothing more than sheets of cardboard, though the muscles in his upper arms attested to their actual weight. She had to drag the things step by step whenever she wanted to move them. Having a strong man to help around the store would be a blessing. Charlie had been a faithful employee, but he was a slightly built, thoughtful man who would rather help the customers than wrestle the boxes in the stockroom.

A few minutes later, Ethan stopped in the door, tapping lightly on the frame to get her attention. "The tables are up."

"Thank you. I'll show you where the other things are in a moment."

He nodded. "I didn't see a time clock or a sign-out sheet anyplace. How do you want me to keep track of my hours?"

"Oh. We use the honor system. Arrive at nine unless we've made other arrangements. An hour for lunch. Leave at six. Same with overtime. You tell me what you worked, I'll pay you for it."

"You must have had trusted employees in the past."

"I did." She hoped that she could trust him, as well.

His eyes warmed again, and the corner of his mouth moved. Without a word, he patted the door frame lightly and turned away, only to turn back again and catch her gaze. "You can trust me, Ms. Latimer."

"Nicki. You can call me Nicki."

He smiled. "Nicki it is."

Nicki blinked, unable to look away. He'd smiled. A heart-stopping, knee-weakening, melt-your-insides smile that created deep creases at the corners of his mouth and revealed strong white teeth made more dazzling against his tanned skin. She swallowed through the sudden dryness in her throat, feeling dazed and warm all over.

He disappeared down the hall, and she released a pent-up breath, fanning herself with her hands to ease the heat in her cheeks. A moment later, she heard the thump of a box landing on the floor and the whiz of a utility knife slicing through tape. A sense of confidence washed through her—something she hadn't felt for a very long time. She'd made a good decision hiring Ethan. Hopefully it was the first of many more. If she could collect enough good decisions, maybe they would bury the one horrible one she'd made when she'd married Brad.

Ethan rolled his shoulders, wincing at the twinge. His back was sore, his neck ached, and his legs were protesting the stooping and lifting he'd done all morning. But he felt better than he had in months. Honest work. Simple work. And nothing to trigger a memory from his past. All in all, it had been a good morning.

He wasn't sure what had triggered his small flashback yesterday. Perhaps seeing the soldier or anxiety over joining a new PTSD group. Thankfully he'd been able to hold off the images. This time.

He could hear Nicki in the front of the store, her voice warm and pleasant as she waited on a customer. She had a way of making each person feel that their business was appreciated. He was going to like working here. He liked working for Nicki. She was a confident, capable woman. Yet there was also something fragile about her, as if her determination and confidence could shatter at any moment. Nicki Latimer was an interesting combination of strength and softness.

Her vulnerability triggered his protective instincts, something he hadn't felt in a long time. And noticing an attractive woman made him feel human again. He'd spent too much time trying to survive. It was nice to experience normal reactions again.

Ethan pried the shipping label from a small box, turning to glance at Nicki as she strode into the stockroom and went to the storage closet. Sliding the blade back into the box cutter, he watched as she rummaged through the shelves a moment, then pulled out a new lightbulb, shut the cabinet and reached for the four-foot folding stepladder leaning against the wall.

She smiled over her shoulder, holding up the bulb. "Light's out in my office."

"Need some help?"

"No. I can do it myself."

He watched her walk away, lugging the awkward stool, her shoulders squared. The defiant tone in her voice piqued his curiosity. Maybe he should keep an eye on her. He wasn't comfortable with her climbing an old step stool without someone to steady it.

He found her in her office, stool unfolded and placed

squarely beneath the light fixture. The office ceiling was at least ten feet. To reach the socket she'd have to stand on the top step, and even then it would be a stretch. He stepped forward, extending his hand. "Let me do that."

She pulled the lightbulb out of his reach, her blue eyes darkening to navy. "Don't tell me what to do. I'm perfectly capable of changing a lightbulb."

Ethan held her gaze, surprised to see fear flash through her blue eyes. Her posture was rigid. Her jaw was set. He held her eyes a moment longer, wishing he could understand and help somehow. But right now, discretion was called for. He stepped to the front of the ladder, steadying it with both hands, and waited.

Slowly, the tension eased from her shoulders. She inhaled a deep breath and grasped the side of the ladder, bulb in the other hand. The front bell chimed, halting her on the first step. She glanced from the doorway back to him, clearly torn between completing her task and greeting the new customer.

He held out his hand. "I'll finish up here. If that's okay." His offer was rewarded with a sweet smile that sent his heart on an odd roller-coaster ride.

"Thanks."

Ethan watched her hurry away, then quickly replaced the lightbulb and returned the step stool to the stockroom. His curiosity about his new boss was fully engaged now. He wanted to know what had caused the fear in her blue eyes. Whatever it was, he'd be keeping a close eye on her from now on. She was prone to acts of recklessness.

A loud rumble from his stomach an hour later reminded Ethan that it was lunchtime. While Nicki had insisted they were on the honor system, he wanted to at least notify her he was leaving. He decided to try the deli around the corner today.

Striding out of the stockroom, he peeked in the office door. It was empty, but he could hear her speaking softly in the back room. He grinned, tugging on his earlobe. Maybe she was the kind who talked to herself. Another thing that made her interesting.

He heard her giggle before she stepped back into the office. He looked over at her, teasing words on the tip of his tongue. He froze. Blood drained from his face. His heart refused to beat. Ice filled his veins.

Nicki stood in the middle of the office with an infant in her arms. She cradled the baby against her shoulder, patting its back and cooing sweetly. Ethan recoiled at the image. His vision flickered between the woman and child in front of him and the woman and child in Afghanistan. One minute together. The next... Claws of horror pierced the back of his mind. He tried to focus on Nicki and the baby, but the image of the others on the ground—broken, torn—intruded. He was sucked back to a dusty street in Afghanistan. He couldn't breathe, couldn't move or even think.

"Oh, Ethan. I want you to meet my daughter, Sadie."

Her voice penetrated his senses slowly like molasses dripping from a spoon. He had to get away. Now. "Yeah. I'm...lunch."

"Ethan. Are you all right?"

Ethan looked from Nicki's proud smile to the little child, with its bobbing fists and little head that wobbled slightly. His stomach twisted. The claws dug deeper, pulling him back. He managed a nod and stumbled back. "I'd better..."

He pivoted and burst out the back door to the parking area behind the stores, stopping in the middle and bending over, resting his hands on his thighs as he drew deep breaths into his lungs. *God help me.* After a few moments, he felt the panic ease. He straightened and raked his fingers across his scalp. His gaze drifted upward, landing on a white steeple visible above the row of brick buildings. The sun glinted off the copper finial, sending rays of light outward.

The Lord is my shepherd. He inhaled, reciting the psalm silently as he concentrated on taking slow measured breaths. By the time he got to *Thy rod and thy staff,* his heart rate was returning to normal, but his gut was still in knots. Lunch was out of the question. Being around people was impossible.

He walked to his car, climbed in and drove the few miles out of Dover to his motel room. Safely inside, he fell on the bed and tried to sort out what to do next. He couldn't stay at the store. He couldn't work there every day seeing Nicki and the baby. He'd go mad. All the work he'd put in over the past year would be gone.

There was only one solution. He had to quit. Today. He wanted to call her immediately and tell her, but he couldn't walk out in the middle of the day. Not after promising her he'd be around to help her redo the store. He'd fight through the rest of the afternoon, but at six tonight he'd tell her he was done. He hated to see the disappointment in her blue eyes, but he had no choice.

He looked at Ron's card, lying on the bedside table. He could call. Talk it out. But his emotions were too raw. He needed time to process what he was feeling. At the very least, time to calm down.

Service. He had to think of his last few hours as service. Then he could get through it. Doing for others had been how he'd gotten through it the first time. That, along with prayer and talking to Paul.

Feeling in control once more, he picked up his keys and headed back. All he had to do was make it through a couple of hours. So much for Dover being the refuge he'd hoped for.

Chapter Three

The incident with Ethan replayed in Nicki's mind as she carried her daughter to the kitchen and prepared a bottle. When she'd seen him in the office doorway, she'd been anxious to show off her beautiful little girl. But instead of the smile and compliments she normally received, Ethan had stared at her and Sadie with a look of shock and horror. He'd paled, and his eyes had glazed over, as if he were seeing something else. He'd mumbled something about lunch, then bolted.

There was no explanation she could think of for his odd behavior. Maybe he didn't like children. Or maybe he'd lost a child and seeing Sadie had reminded him of his loss. Had she made another foolish mistake in hiring him? Maybe her mother was right after all. He'd provided only the barest of information on his job application. Social Security number and a birthdate that made him thirty-three as of a few months ago.

He'd listed his college, but not his degree. Why wouldn't you want people to know what you'd done before? Maybe he had a criminal past. She should have done a background check on him first. She thought back to all the times her husband had kept secrets from her. She'd ignored her instincts and paid a huge price for it.

Brad had always made her feel off balance and uncertain. She didn't get the same sense from Ethan. She snuggled Sadie a little closer against her. "I don't think there's anything sinister about Ethan, do you, sweetheart?" Mysterious maybe, and private, but she always felt safe around him. Something she hadn't felt in a long time. She told herself to forget the incident. But she couldn't dismiss the darkness she'd seen in his eyes.

With her daughter fed and happy, she put her down for tummy time, adjusted the volume on the baby monitor, then went out into the store. The bell hadn't jingled once in the past forty-five minutes. But business was always slow on Mondays. Today that would work to her advantage. She wanted to have this sale set up and the sign posted. Maybe she could lure some bargain hunters in before the store closed.

As always, Ethan had completed his work. The lower shelves had been removed, and the tables were in place. All she had to do was put out the merchandise and pray it would sell quickly.

Taking the roll of tape and a pair of scissors from the drawer at the sales counter, she carried the long, colorful sale sign she'd dug out earlier and moved to the old-fashioned raised display window, using a small stool to step onto the platform. The sign was bulky and awkward. She was struggling with the tape when the bell chimed and Debi walked in.

"You having a sale?"

Nicki lowered the sign and nodded. "Yes. A clearance sale. I've got to get rid of all this old stuff so I can bring in new merchandise. Things people go to Sawyer's Bend or Jackson for. I want to keep them here in Dover."

Debi's smiled brightened. "Sounds like a good idea."

Nicki stepped down from the window and sighed. "But first I have to put up this sign and I can't reach it." She laid the sign and tape on the shelf. "I'll have to have Ethan do it when he gets back from lunch."

"Ethan?" Debi's eyebrows arched.

"The guy I hired Saturday."

Debi went still, her gaze directed toward the back of the store. "You mean him?"

Nicki looked around and saw Ethan approaching. As he came closer, she noticed his stiff shoulders and unreadable expression. He was suppressing his emotions. Something she was familiar with. Had seeing Sadie caused that, or had something else happened? She forced a smile, then introduced Debi. Ethan nodded, keeping his hands at his sides.

"Do you need help with that?" He glanced at the sign lying on the window shelf.

"Yes, thank you." She picked up the tape and scissors and held them out to him. He took the tape first, his fingers brushing against hers and causing her breath to catch. She looked into his eyes to see if he'd felt something too, but his gaze was unreadable and his jaw was set in a hard line. When he lifted the scissors from her grasp, he touched only the handles. "Uh, I'd like it draped through the middle of the window."

Inside the window area, he secured one side, then the other. Nicki watched his progress closely, telling herself she wanted to make sure he did it properly, but keenly aware that she couldn't take her eyes off of him. Ethan moved with a fluid male grace that was pleasing to watch.

With the sale sign perfectly placed, Ethan stepped

down from the display window and handed her the tape and scissors. "Anything else?"

"Thank you." She tried to hold his gaze a moment to show her appreciation, but he looked away. "There are three boxes on the top shelf in the back corner of the stockroom. They probably have the word *Keep* written on the side. If you'll bring those out, I'll add them to the sales table."

He nodded. "Nice to meet you, Ms. Gordon." He walked off.

Debi sighed. "Yummy."

"Hush. He might hear you."

"Like he doesn't know he's dreamy?"

Nicki doubted it. He struck her as the type who would be embarrassed if someone called him "dreamy."

Debi nudged her arm. "I want to know all about him."

So did she. For a moment, she considered telling her friend about Ethan's odd reaction to Sadie, but decided against it for now.

"You know, Nicki…" Debi nodded thoughtfully. "If you wanted to really increase business, all you'd have to do is have him stand in the front window. I'll bet your sales would go through the roof."

Nicki shook her head. "Oh, come on." She noticed Ethan returning with two of the boxes and quickly changed the subject. "If you stopped by to see Sadie, she's napping."

"No, I came by to see if you'd heard about the break-in last night?"

"Another one?" She stepped aside to let Ethan place the cartons on the sale table, catching a whiff of his enticing aftershave. She forced her attention on Debi. "Where?"

"Durrant's Hardware. They took the computer, some

petty cash and several expensive power tools. That's the fourth store to be broken into in the last two weeks."

A twinge of alarm chased down Nicki's spine. She'd worked late several nights since taking over the store. Now the thought of being here alone with the baby didn't sound like a good idea. Her gaze shifted to Ethan as he walked away. Of course, with him here she'd feel perfectly safe. His muscular build and stern demeanor would no doubt deter any burglar who tried to break in. "Do the police have any leads?"

"Nothing solid yet." Debi rested one hand below her throat. "I'm glad it's still light out when I leave work. Otherwise I'd have Jerry take me home in his patrol car every night."

Nicki studied her friend, noting the worry in her usually bright blue eyes. "How are you dealing with Jerry's new job as a police officer?"

"Okay, I guess. I try not to think about it. There's not much crime in Dover. At least not until these robberies started." She shrugged. "But I do worry. I've met a few of the other officers' wives. Captain Durrant's wife, Ginger, is new to life as a law-enforcement spouse. We've talked a couple of times. It helps."

"I'm glad. You know I'll be praying for his safety."

"Thanks." Debi pulled her into a warm hug. "I miss you, Nicki. Before Sadie was born and your dad had his transplant, we used to have lunch and go shopping. Now we can only manage to steal a few minutes during the day."

"I know. I miss that, too. But by the end of the day, I'm too tired to do anything but fall into bed. And you're not exactly a stay-at-home mom."

"I know. Carter and Zoe have both started soccer. I

feel like I'm on the road nonstop. Promise me we'll do lunch or dinner soon."

"Promise."

Nicki watched her friend leave and realized how much her life had changed since coming home. At times she felt trapped and alone, unable to break free to live her own life. While she loved her parents and was grateful for their help, she was completely dependent on them for everything. Even her job. The only thing that kept her going was knowing that eventually she and Sadie could leave Dover and start over.

The afternoon passed more quickly than she'd anticipated, allowing her to forget for brief moments about her meeting with her friend the accountant. A glance at the clock showed it was almost closing time. Gary would be here soon. As she walked back to her office, her gaze drifted to the stockroom. Ethan had kept to himself most of the afternoon. His reaction to Sadie still nagged at her mind, but she couldn't bring herself to ask him about it.

She glanced up at the bright light illuminating her desk. She owed Ethan an apology. He'd tried to help her with the bulb. But his "Let me do that" statement had triggered something in her, and she'd lashed out. She wasn't about to let anyone tell her what to do. She was perfectly capable of taking care of herself. But that didn't justify rudeness.

Nicki went in search of her new employee and found him out front, replenishing stock. He turned, bracing his shoulders, his eyes guarded. Did he think she was going to press him about his reaction earlier?

She chewed her lip a moment, preparing her speech. "I'm sorry about the lightbulb thing. I know you were just trying to help."

He picked up the carton he'd emptied and folded the flaps inward. His gaze met hers. "No problem. I like to do things for myself, too."

How had he interpreted her behavior so correctly? The look in his eyes led her to believe he truly did understand. All of her life, people had been telling her to stop being so bullheaded and independent. No one understood the satisfaction she found in achieving things on her own.

"Well, I appreciate your help. Thanks."

He nodded. "That's what I'm here for."

Nicki went back to her office. Ethan was right. She'd hired him to help. Tomorrow she would train him on the register. But today, she had to deal with Gary's findings.

Picking up the new floor plan she'd sketched out for the store, she studied it again. Her training in marketing told her the plan to revitalize Latimer's was sound, but as a daughter, she feared her plan might fail and cost her parents their business. If only she knew for sure. Her confidence was so fragile. One minute she thought she could conquer the world. The next, humiliation and shame would drag her back down into feelings of powerlessness and defeat. She couldn't trust her own judgment, not after the mistakes she'd made.

"Nicki."

She looked up to find Ethan in the office doorway. "There's someone here to see you."

He moved aside, and Gary Palmer stepped into the office. "Hey, Nichelle."

Gary hadn't changed much since high school. He was short and stocky with a head of unruly red hair, and his boyish grin eased some of her anxiety.

She rose and greeted him with a hug. "It's good to see you."

"It's good to have you home again."

Nicki glanced over his shoulder and saw Ethan watching her from the stockroom. The hard look on his face puzzled her, until she realized he was gauging the situation, watching out for her. The protective gesture pleased her. It was nice to have someone looking out for her. As long as it didn't go too far.

Closing the office door, she gave her full attention to Gary. Seated at her desk, she took a deep breath. "How bad is it?"

Gary laid a folder on the desk and opened it. "Of course, I can only report on the information you gave me, but it appears that your father has been juggling accounts for some time to keep the store running."

"What about the lump sum he deposited? Where did that come from?"

"Without access to the personal accounts, I can't say, but I'd guess he's tapped out his savings or mortgaged the house."

"Bottom line?"

"Unless something changes, the store can limp along for six months, maybe a year, and then…" He shrugged. "I'm sorry. I wish I had better news."

After Gary left, Nicki cradled her head between her hands, her thoughts tumbling with the news he'd delivered. Things were worse than she'd thought. Unless something changed, the store was facing bankruptcy within the next few months. Her father's infusion of cash helped, but once the outstanding bills were taken care of, there wouldn't be much left to upgrade the merchandise. Her grand plan was out of the question now. How had her father let things get so bad? And how was she going to keep it from getting worse?

Insecurity and doubt washed over her like a wave on

the beach, sucking her confidence out from under her. A tidal wave of emotions swelled in her chest, but she had no strength left to fight them. Laying her head on her arms, she gave in and cried.

Ethan tossed the utility knife onto the worktable in the stockroom. Six o'clock. Time to leave. Time to tell Nicki Latimer he was quitting. He took a deep breath, resting his hands on his hips. His resolve had wavered slightly since this morning after he'd overheard Nicki's friend telling her about the burglaries in town. A woman with a baby working alone at night wasn't a good idea. He didn't know Nicki well, but he'd learned enough to know she'd stay until her work was done, no matter how late the hour.

Those protective instincts that had been triggered early were growing. But that wasn't his problem. Nicki wasn't his problem. Nicki and Sadie together were the issue. He'd managed to keep busy all afternoon, and the few times he'd wandered out into the main part of the store, he'd been able to concentrate on his task and nothing else. Unless Nicki was there. Then he'd had to battle the wish to watch her while she worked. Another reason to leave. The lovely store manager messed with his mind. Thankfully, the baby hadn't been with her those times or he would have had a different reaction. He'd heard the little one crying once, but that hadn't bothered him. It was seeing the two of them together that would trigger the horror.

He wondered about the man who had stopped by. She'd hugged him like an old friend. Was there something more than friendship between them? A prick of unreasonable jealousy lodged in his chest. The man hadn't stayed long, but the look on his face when he'd left suggested something serious.

Ethan rubbed his forehead. He had to remind himself that Nicki wasn't his concern. His sanity was. The dark memories he'd locked away were trying to break free, threatening to pull him under again. He couldn't stay. Scooping up his jacket, he set his jaw and headed toward the office. Best to end this quickly. She'd find more help soon enough.

He heard muffled sounds as he stepped to the threshold of the office. He looked in and his throat tightened. Nicki had her head down on the desk, sobbing. Her soft groans and sniffles pierced his heart. Had something hurt her? The baby? He glanced toward the back room, but he found no clues.

"Nicki?"

She gasped, but kept her head down.

"Are you all right? What happened?"

Slowly, she raised her head, keeping her gaze averted and swiveling her chair to keep from looking at him directly. "I'm fine."

Clearly she wasn't. He stepped into the office, stopping in front of her desk. "Beautiful women don't cry when they're fine." That got her attention. She looked at him, wiping tears from her cheeks.

"I got some bad news today."

"The man who was here?"

"Yes. He's an old friend. An accountant."

Snagging a folding chair, he opened it and sat. "And?" She wanted to tackle life alone. He recognized the symptoms.

Nicki looked away. "Nothing. I don't want to talk about it."

"Bad idea. Talking about a difficult situation is the

only way to get past the problem." She stared at him, and he could see her contemplating his suggestion. She shook her head and pulled a tissue from a drawer to wipe her nose.

"I have to save the store." She kept her eyes on the tissue she was twisting in her hands.

He leaned forward, elbows resting on his knees. "Save it from what?" An uneasy feeling formed in his gut.

Her shoulders sagged abruptly, as if she'd lost all strength in her body. "Bankruptcy."

Ethan forced his features to remain neutral and not reveal his surprise. Nicki needed to get this off her chest. The least he could do was listen before he walked out.

"Is that what the accountant told you?"

She slipped her fingers through her hair, grasping it at the back of her neck before letting it go. It fell in tangled strands across her shoulders, and he found himself wondering what her hair would feel like in his hands.

"He only confirmed what I've suspected for some time. The store is failing. I should have paid closer attention. I was dealing with…personal issues. I had a feeling something was wrong, but I didn't want to know. Now I've got to find a way to keep this place going. It's my parents' only source of income."

"Why is that up to you? Why aren't they here helping you?"

"My father is recuperating from a kidney transplant. My mother is caring for him. When I came home after… they asked me to work at the store. Of course I said I would. I was pregnant with Sadie, but it was so nice to be busy again." She sniffed. "Then Sadie was born, and Dad found a donor, and Charlie had to stay on to run the store until I could come back, and then he left, and now it's all up to me."

He tried to connect all the dots in her explanation, but one thing was certain: she was in over her head. "So your plan to change the store—moving fixtures around, bringing in new stock, giving it a hipper image—is your attempt to save Latimer's for your parents."

Nicki's blue eyes darkened. "Yes. And it's a good plan."

He wanted to smile at her defensiveness, but didn't figure that was a wise move. "It *is* a good plan. I think it'll work."

She blinked her eyes, still moist from tears. "You do?"

Her lack of confidence surprised him. She'd been clear and precise about what she wanted done. So why the doubt all of a sudden? "I do. But you can't do it all by yourself. You need help."

"I have you."

But he was here to quit. He couldn't stay and risk dredging up the darkness again. He might not survive a second time. "Yeah. If you don't mind me asking, where is your husband? I would have thought he'd be here helping out."

Her expression went from worried to closed off in an instant.

"Dead."

The hollow look in her eyes hit Ethan like a blow. Nicki had been through something terrible.

She clasped her hands in front of her on the desk. "I know my plan will work, and with your help, I'm sure we can change the way people think about Latimer's, and business will pick up, and by the time Dad is ready to come back to work it'll be back on its feet. Then

Sadie and I can leave." She stopped, staring at the desktop before looking up again. "Well, it *was* a good plan."

Leave? Was she planning on moving away from Dover? "What do you mean?"

She stared at the report. "My father didn't tell me the whole story. Gary suspects Dad has been robbing Peter to pay Paul. Once I settle all the outstanding accounts, there won't be enough money to redesign the store. I'll have to work with what's left, but I doubt that'll be enough to turn things around."

Ethan nodded and crossed his arms over his chest. "Sounds like time for plan B."

"I don't have a plan B."

Her bottom lip quivered, filling him with a desire to pull her into his arms. "But you will."

She met his gaze, her blue eyes wide. "How do you know that?"

"Because you made a plan A. You don't strike me as someone who gives up easily."

She looked away, fidgeting with the papers on her desk as if uncomfortable with his observation. "I'm just tired, that's all. Sadie was up a lot last night, and I didn't get much sleep. Things will look better tomorrow."

Ethan tensed. He needed to get this over with. "Tomorrow."

He saw her mentally gird herself. She looked up at him, her usual smile once more shining through. He doubted if anything could keep her down for long.

"Did you want to talk to me about something?"

He looked at her, his heart softening at the hopeful light in her eyes. Her face was a bit puffy, her nose pink, her mouth pulled into a small frown. Her vulnerability touched something deep inside him. She was counting on him to help her save her parents' store. But he couldn't. He thought about seeing her with the baby this morning and his gut twisted. He stood, sending the metal chair scraping along the floor. He couldn't stay here. Period. But how could he leave her in the lurch like this? He opened his mouth to say the words, but then he remembered the robberies. He couldn't leave them here alone. Which meant he couldn't leave. Dragging a hand across the back of his neck, he sent up a prayer for strength and guidance. "So what do you want to tackle tomorrow?"

Nicki smiled, and the sun came out. "Come up with a plan B?"

"Sure thing." He started to leave, then turned back. "You heading out soon? I don't think it's a good idea for you and…the little one to hang around here alone." What if she worked late and the robbers showed up? He'd never forgive himself if anything happened to them. For some reason he didn't understand, he felt responsible for them. Maybe because they were alone like him and no one else seemed to care.

She nodded. "I'm leaving right now. Thanks for listening, Ethan."

He puttered around in the stockroom until she was ready to leave, then followed her out, keeping his gaze averted from the sight of her and the baby as she secured the infant in its car seat. He took his time getting into his car, making sure she was safely inside hers and driving away before he cranked the engine on his Malibu.

He leaned back in the driver's seat, his heart beating double time. How was he going to do this? The Lord had thrown him a giant curveball. He'd wanted his new life in Dover to be simple; he'd wanted it to be a place where he could learn to manage his emotions and live in the moment. But now he didn't know how he would get through the next few minutes, let alone remain here and work for weeks. Somehow he had to find a way to help Nicki, but avoid seeing her and the baby together.

Pulling out his phone, he scrolled through his contacts until Paul's name appeared. He needed some advice, and he needed it fast.

Chapter Four

The gate blocking the railroad track slowly lifted and the line of cars crept forward. Ethan tapped the steering wheel as he waited, trying to maintain his composure and not let his nerves get the better of him.

If he had any sense, he'd call Nicki, tell her goodbye and move on. He'd spent last night questioning his decision, but always coming to the same conclusion. He couldn't leave Nicki to run that store alone. Unfortunately, these thoughts had unleashed old nightmares. The only difference had been the endings. While they used to end with the explosion, then blackness, last night they'd ended with Nicki and the baby running away. From him. Maybe that was progress.

He knew better than to assign any significance to the dreams. They were only subconscious fears mixed up with his PTSD-scrambled brain. The real threat today would be doing his job and keeping a lock on his memories.

Nicki's car was already parked behind the store when he pulled in. He went inside, hoping to slip into the stockroom unnoticed and get to work. But as he moved down the hallway, he heard conversation coming from the office. Wanting to make sure everything was all right, he stepped to the open door and glanced in.

Nicki was cradling the baby in her arms, talking softly, her back to him as she gave the little one her bottle. He ducked back out of sight, but couldn't help overhearing as she talked to her daughter.

"I'm sorry that you don't have a daddy, sweetie. Mommy really messed up on that. I wanted you to have a daddy like me. Someone to love you no matter what, who'll think you're special, someone to protect you. But your daddy wasn't like that. Which is why we had to get away. So it's just you and me, Sadie. But we'll be okay. I promise."

Ethan slowly backed up, then made his way to the kitchen. What had she meant by "get away"? What had happened between her and her husband? Questions multiplied in his head.

Pouring a cup of coffee, he stared at the dark liquid, relieved that seeing Nicki and the baby today hadn't triggered any memories. He released a slow breath. Perhaps yesterday's reaction had been a result of surprise. But he'd still have to be on guard. The threat of a flashback lurked in the shadows of his mind like a mountain lion poised to attack.

"Good morning." Nicki joined him at the coffeemaker. "I thought I heard you come in."

He glanced at her briefly before spooning sugar into his coffee. "Where's the little one?"

"I put her down for some tummy time."

Ethan had no idea what that meant. His expression must have given him away.

"She's playing."

Nicki reached across him for a cup, surrounding him with the scents of gardenias and baby powder. The light from the ceiling fixture danced off her yellow hair, making it shimmer as she moved. She grasped the coffee carafe and he couldn't help but notice her small hands. He allowed his gaze to skim over her. The print dress she wore nipped in at her waist and flared softly over her hips. The word *delicate* came to mind. But even though Nicki may appear delicate, he knew underneath she was a woman made of strong determination and grit. He returned his focus to the coffee in his cup and not the lovely woman beside him.

"Ethan, about yesterday…"

He braced before turning to look at her. Curiosity reflected in her eyes. He did *not* want to talk about his reaction or explain about his PTSD. He'd learned the hard way that it triggered fear and distrust in many people.

"I want to apologize. I was an emotional mess and unloaded on you. My only excuse is that I wasn't prepared for the news my friend gave me."

He stared. That was what she wanted to talk about? The tension in his shoulders eased. "You have a lot on your plate right now."

"True, but what I need is action, not tears. I've got to stay focused on my goal."

"What goal is that?"

"Getting out of Dover."

Disappointment settled heavily on his shoulders. He'd barely come to know her and she was making plans to leave. An old ache resurfaced. No one in his life stayed for long. They were all only temporary. Apparently Nicki would be another one on his long, long list.

"Which brings me to another subject." She took a sip of her coffee, looking at him above the rim. His heart caught in his throat. "I'd like to train you on the cash register today. With all the paperwork, and keeping an eye on Sadie, it would be a big help if we could both handle customers."

He added creamer to his cup, watching the dark coffee turn a caramel color. He'd hoped this part of his job wouldn't come until later. Why had he ever thought working here would be simple? Two days in and he was facing all the things he'd wanted to avoid.

He glanced at her briefly. "I'm not much of a salesman. I'm more of a behind-the-scenes kind of guy."

"You'd be my backup, not a full-time salesperson. It would help me out a lot."

The hopeful look in her eyes punctured his reluctance. He'd promised himself when he'd come to Dover he'd step out, embrace life. Here was his first test. "Okay. Sure."

"Great. I'll go get the till and we'll do it right now. And don't worry about helping the customers. Everyone here in Dover is friendly. Just flash that great smile of yours and the customers will be happy. Meet me out front when you're done with your coffee." She hurried out of the kitchen.

Ethan stared after her. She thought he had a great smile? He let that thought settle for a few moments before joining Nicki at the register. He looked over her shoulder, inhaling the gardenia scent again and fighting to keep his mind on her words and not the way his senses reacted to being near her.

"It's a simple system. I don't think you'll have much trouble learning it. It pretty much runs itself."

She ran through the steps, letting him count the till and practice a few sales and returns and closing out at the end of the day. She smiled, brushing the bangs off her forehead. "You're a quick learner." She patted his arm. "I knew you would be."

The warmth of her hand seeped through the fabric of his shirt and traveled along every nerve in his body. He nodded, finding it hard to pull his gaze from her sweet smile. She looked into his eyes for a moment, then stepped back.

"There's a shipment of fashion cell-phone covers coming in this morning that I think the teens will love. I want to get them on the floor quickly. I'll let you know where I want to display them and give you the price point later."

"I'll keep an eye out for it."

Once he was back in the stockroom, Ethan took a deep breath, struggling to dispel the lingering effects of Nicki's nearness. She evoked feelings he'd ignored for a long time. Feelings that had no place in his life right now. But he just couldn't walk away and leave her in the lurch.

When he'd talked with Paul last night, his friend had reminded him to focus on service, and that was what he intended to do. Paul had also reminded him that avoidance was not the way to deal with his situation. He prayed he was right because he'd taken another step deeper into Nicki's life. Letting Nicki down was a more distasteful prospect than facing her and the baby. But he'd have to keep his barriers up. Something about Nicki penetrated his defenses and he wasn't sure he could let it go.

Nicki hung up the phone, sighed, silently gave a prayer of thanks and then leaned back in her chair. She'd negotiated new payment plans with most of her father's vendors, which would give her breathing space for the next few months. Of course, that didn't put a dent in the bill for the supplier who had suspended shipments or cover the merchandise she'd already ordered before she'd known the extent of the store's financial trouble. She suspected her dad had tapped out his savings to keep the store going, which worried her, but also made her more determined than ever to save the store.

Soft gurgles from the other room told her Sadie was awake. Lifting her daughter from the crib, she held her close, kissing her little head. Her baby girl was particularly cuddly when she woke up. "How's my sweet girl? Did you have happy dreams?" After putting a fresh diaper and a new polka-dot onesie on Sadie, Nicki placed her in the bouncy chair on her desk. She liked to keep her close so she could talk to her and touch her while she worked. It wasn't an ideal situation, but she couldn't bear to let her out of her sight. She touched Sadie's hand, smiling when the little fingers curled around her index finger.

A faint noise drew her attention and she paused, listening for the bell on the front door of the store. When it didn't come, she sighed, tapping Sadie's toes lightly. "Business is slow today, sweetie." Her early back-to-school sale had gone well, but she needed more foot traffic if she was going to turn business around. She needed to place an ad in the *Dover Dispatch* and let people know Latimer's was having a makeover.

Now that Ethan knew how to work the register, she could take more time to come up with ideas. The thought buoyed her spirits. He'd suggested a plan B, but she'd been too busy, and too stunned by Gary's report, to even consider one.

Nicki tried to go back to work, but it was hard to concentrate when all she wanted to do was hold her precious little girl. She never dreamed she'd feel this way. She'd searched her whole life for a place where she fit, a purpose, and she'd found it in one tiny person.

She thanked God every hour for her sweet Sadie. The love she felt was so powerful, sometimes she feared she couldn't hold it all inside.

By noon, Nicki had come up with a dozen ideas to revitalize the store on a small budget and discarded all of them. What she needed was someone to brainstorm with.

When she heard a light tapping on the door frame, she looked up and saw Ethan standing there, filling the space with his broad shoulders and long legs. He certainly was an attractive man, though a man of mystery.

He slipped his hands into the back pockets of his jeans. "I'm heading out for lunch."

She reminded herself to take advantage of the resources at hand. "Ethan, I could use your help with something."

"Name it."

She chewed her lip a moment. "Plan B."

He raised his eyebrows. "Okay. What exactly do you need?"

"A plan B."

A full-blown smile appeared on his face, softening the sharp angles, turning his dark eyes to warm cocoa and easing the squared-off shoulders into a curved position. "Let me go get one from the stockroom for you."

Nicki blinked at his unexpected teasing. In the few days he'd been at the store, he'd rarely smiled and never revealed a lighthearted side at all. She liked this side of Ethan Stone. "I wish it were that simple."

"I'm not sure how I can help."

Nicki looked away. The compassion in his dark eyes was having an odd effect on her nerves. "I need to brainstorm ideas with someone—ways to revamp the store without a lot of money. With running the store and taking care of Sadie—" she bit her lip "—I'm not thinking as logically as I usually do."

"All right. My brain could use a challenge."

"Thanks. I brought enough lunch today to feed a baseball team. We could talk while we eat, unless you have plans."

"Nope, no plans."

"Good. Well, give me a minute and I'll get it all set up." He nodded and walked away. Nicki expelled a pent-up breath she hadn't realized she'd been holding. Being around Ethan always left her feeling like a teenager with a crush on the new boy in school. Ridiculous. Besides, there was a dark, edgy quality about him that made her uneasy. But then he'd do something thoughtful and she'd catch a glimpse of a different Ethan. Her curiosity grew by the moment, even though she'd sensed that, like her, he had things in his life he had no desire to share.

That should have given her comfort. She wouldn't have to worry about him asking her questions, digging up old pains. But strangely it only made her more curious about her strong and silent employee.

Pushing up from her chair, she checked on Sadie, leaving the door open in case the baby woke, then headed for the kitchen. She'd pulled out the containers filled with roast beef and homemade noodles from last night. Ethan entered the kitchen as she removed a pitcher of sweet tea from the old fridge. Suddenly the front bell sounded. "I'd better go see. Go ahead and help yourself."

When she returned, the table was set with the old plastic plates she kept in the cupboard, paper napkins and glasses of iced tea. Ethan was at the sink, wiping his hands with a paper towel. "Wow. I guess you know your way around a kitchen."

He joined her at the table. "A single man has to acquire some culinary skills."

After filling their plates, Ethan closed his eyes briefly for a prayer. The gesture brought up another question. Ethan must be a Christian. Something Brad hadn't been. At one time she hadn't thought it mattered, but now faith was at the top of her list for next time. Not that there would be a next time. She would never give her heart over to another man. The risk was too high.

She glanced over at Ethan, questions growing like the kudzu in the fields outside of Dover. She wished she knew more about him. "Do you have any family, Ethan?"

He stopped in midbite, wiping his mouth with the napkin. "No."

Her cheeks flamed. "Sorry. I didn't mean to pry."

He held her gaze a moment, his dark eyes probing. "My mother died in a car accident when I was eight. I was raised in foster care."

Sadness squeezed her heart at the thought of him growing up alone, shifted from one place to the other. Words of sympathy lay on the tip of her tongue, but the tension she saw in his shoulders stopped the impulse.

"This plan B. What exactly do you need?" Ethan asked her.

Suddenly, confiding in a stranger—her employee— seemed like a bad move. Her mother would be horrified if she knew Nicki was discussing personal troubles with Ethan. But looking at the compassion in Ethan's eyes, Nicki set her reservations aside. Her priority now was saving the store.

"I had hoped to buy new display fixtures, rework the floor plan and bring in updated merchandise. We've carried the same items in this store for years. I think business would improve if I could offer items customers want today. Like tablets, laptops, smartphones and business software."

Ethan was pensive for a moment, then said, "I've looked at the fixtures, and from what I can see, they're modular. They could be reassembled into a new configuration without too much trouble. All that's really needed is a new coat of paint."

Nicki's hope rose a notch. "Really? That would save a lot of money. Maybe we could paint the walls a brighter color." She sighed. "Now if I could find a way to get rid of those old computers and replace them with laptops and tablets."

Ethan frowned at her across the small table. "You have more of those tower dinosaurs like the one on display?" He cleared his throat. "Sorry. But no one uses those anymore."

Nicki nodded. "I know. And yes, I have five of them upstairs that I couldn't give away if my life depended on it. And in a way, it does. I can't restart my life until I get this place back on solid ground."

Ethan rested his elbows on the table, hands lightly clasped. "You're anxious to leave Dover?"

"As soon as I get the estate settled, Sadie and I are starting our lives fresh, someplace *I* choose." She realized she'd said the words with more intensity than she'd intended and she could sense Ethan's curiosity. "There are legal issues with my husband's estate." She hoped he wouldn't press for more, and he didn't. But there was a sympathetic light in his eyes that soothed her. Odd. Sometimes his look said more than words.

Ethan rubbed his chin. "When I worked at the discount store, the electronics vendors would offer programs where we could return outdated items for upgraded ones."

Nicki inhaled a deep breath. "You're right. Why didn't I think of that?" She pushed back her chair and stood. "I saw a notice the other day, but I dismissed it. Maybe it's not too late." She hurried from the room. In her office, she shuffled through a stack of papers until she found the one she was looking for.

A small gurgle from the back room brought a smile to her face. Sadie was up and ready to eat. Hurrying to the portable crib, Nicki scooped up the tiny girl and cradled her close. "Hello, sweet pea. Did you have a nice nap? Are you hungry?" She kissed the downy hair and was rewarded with waving fists and a smile. She moved to the cabinet she used as a changing table and swapped out the wet diaper for a dry one. "There. That feels better, doesn't it?"

"Let's go eat and see what this letter says. Maybe Mommy can save this old store, and then you and I can skedaddle to a new place all our own." She walked into the kitchen. "Look who's awake."

Ethan looked at Sadie. His eyes darkened, then became distant and glazed over, as if he were a thousand miles away looking at something else, something horrible. There was something familiar about the look, but she couldn't place it. "Ethan. Is something wrong?"

He blinked, and then the glazed look in his eyes was replaced with realization. He rubbed his forehead and looked down at the table. "No. I was just…" He cleared his throat. "Did you find the letter?"

"Yes." She handed it to him. She prepared Sadie's bottle, speaking softly to her as she mixed her formula.

"Looks good, but you'll have to check the dates on the shipments."

Hope chased away her questions about Ethan. "As soon as the store is closed, we'll go upstairs and look."

"Upstairs? Are you talking about those wooden stairs outside behind the store?"

Nicki nodded. "There are two apartments up there, but they haven't been used in ages. Dad didn't like being a landlord. Too many headaches. He had plans to add an inside stairway and expand the second floor into a sales area, but then the recession hit and he shelved the idea."

Nicki shifted Sadie in her arms. "Would you mind watching the store for a few minutes while I feed her?"

Ethan looked as if he would refuse but nodded. "Sure."

Nicki watched him walk away, her mind churning with questions. How could he be so helpful and considerate one moment, then cool and withdrawn the next? She was tempted to ask him, but she doubted he'd explain. Though she understood, it did little to curb her curiosity.

Ethan was surprised at how quickly the afternoon passed. The phone covers had arrived, and he'd set up the display in front near the window. When he wasn't straightening or unpacking merchandise, he jotted down ideas to discuss with Nicki. She was smart. Sure, she would come up with ideas on her own, but he liked helping her and being a part of the store.

"Ethan!"

Her shout made him hurry to the office. "Something wrong?"

"What? No. I just locked up the store, and I thought we'd go upstairs and check out those computers."

"Sure." He noticed that Nicki had donned some kind of harness over her chest. Before he could ask what it was, she stepped into the back room, returning with Sadie. She walked toward him and held out the baby.

"Here. I need help getting her in this thing."

Ethan froze. Every nerve in his body tensed. An image of the other mother and child flashed in the back of his mind, but Nicki was waiting for him to take the child. He had no choice but to grasp the tiny body. His hands completely encircled her small rib cage. Sadie's little fists began to bob and she kicked her legs. Her mouth pulled downward. He realized she was unhappy being dangled in midair.

Slowly he pulled her to him, curling in his left arm and positioning her against his chest. Immediately, her squirming stopped, and her expression returned to one of contentment. She was so small, so soft. Her skin was so delicate he feared his rough hands would hurt her.

He inhaled a sweet scent of baby powder and something else pleasant. Then Sadie looked into his eyes and smiled. A strange warmth seeped into him, turning his heart to liquid and making him smile back.

"I thought you didn't like kids."

Ethan glanced up at Nicki. She looked as surprised as he felt. "I love kids." Sadie's smile had rearranged his insides, and he was finding it hard to process what he was feeling.

Nicki stepped forward and held out her hands.

"Okay, slip her legs in these holes, facing outward, and hold her while I fasten the pouch up."

Ethan did as he was instructed, watching with interest as Nicki secured the baby in the contraption.

"There we go." Nicki kissed Sadie's little head. Retrieving a set of keys from the desk, she smiled at Ethan. "Now we can go and explore the apartments hands free." Outside, she locked the store, then crossed the short distance to the wooden stairs that rose to the second floor. Ethan grasped the railing and gave it a tug. "Are you sure this is safe?"

"It's fine." She started up, holding the rails with both hands as she went. He could appreciate the pouch now. It made things easier for Nicki and safer for Sadie, as well. He followed behind, keeping a watchful eye on mother and child.

At the top of the stairs, Nicki unlocked the steel outer door that opened into a long hallway. "I think the computers are in this rear apartment." Ethan followed her through a door into a room partially filled with boxes, display fixtures and a battered table and chairs. A compact kitchen took up one wall, and through another door he could see a bedroom.

Nicki shook her head. "It's worse than I thought. But like I said, no one has lived here in at least five years."

Ethan moved to the stack of boxes. "Here's your computers." He stooped down and removed the shipping label and handed it to Nicki.

"How many are there?"

"Looks like five. Plus the one downstairs." He stood and looked around at the other boxes. "Do you know what these are?"

She shook her head. "I'll come back later and check them out. I don't think I've been up here in years. Pretty awful, isn't it?"

Ethan glanced around the small apartment. "Just needs a good cleaning and some paint. But it's not bad."

Nicki frowned as she walked out the door and across the hall, selecting another key from the small ring she carried. "Might as well check out the other apartment, too."

Ethan followed behind her as she opened the door

and stepped inside. This apartment was in the front of the store and had the benefit of four large windows that looked out onto the street below.

"Oh, wow. I'd forgotten how pretty those windows are." Nicki walked toward them. "Look at all the light coming in. I don't remember the brick wall being exposed either." She turned and smiled at him, one hand entwined with Sadie's tiny fingers.

His heart stopped midbeat. As far as he was concerned, the only light in the room was her. He swallowed, then felt his heart start beating again. "Have you thought about renting them out? It would be a steady source of income."

"I know, but look at this place. Mauve carpet, wallpaper borders… The cabinets aren't bad, but the light oak is outdated." She walked over to the kitchen, then glanced back to the living area. "You know, if we took this wall down, it would open the space up and even more light could come in."

Ethan peeked into the room on the other side of the living room. "Is this a two-bedroom?"

"There should be a master bedroom in the front and a small one in the back." Sadie sneezed. "Oh, I'd better get her out of here. It's too dusty."

Ethan took the stairs ahead of her as they descended. Back in the office, Nicki placed the packing slip from the computers on the desk. "Hopefully I can find these in Dad's records." She reached out for the keyboard, but typing was awkward with Sadie strapped to her chest.

"Are you going to stay and work late?"

She nodded. "I'd like to get this settled as soon as possible."

"Then I'll stay, too."

"You don't need to do that."

"It's not a good idea…" Remembering Nicki didn't like to be told what to do, he tried to rephrase. "Do you think it's wise to stay here alone, considering what's been happening around town?"

She sighed. "I guess not."

"Besides, how are you going to get the baby out of that contraption without help?"

"Good point."

She came toward him. His gaze traveled from her blue eyes to baby Sadie, who seemed content to watch from the safety of the pouch.

"Hold her while I unfasten it."

He slipped his fingers around Sadie's small chest, taking the weight in his hands as Nicki released the straps. This time he didn't hesitate to pull the baby close. He rested her up against his shoulder, her head bobbing a bit before resting against the side of his cheek. He wasn't a stranger to little kids. There had been plenty of them in his foster homes, but he had little experience with one this young.

Nicki shed the pouch and came to retrieve her daughter. Ethan found himself strangely reluctant to hand her over. The realization stunned him. One smile from this tiny child had shifted his perceptions. As he handed Sadie to her mom, their hands overlapped, and for a moment he experienced a current of awareness unlike anything he'd ever known. They were linked. Man, woman and child. His breath caught in his throat. Nicki took Sadie in her arms, breaking the connection. Once again he saw the same pose, mother cradling infant, but the image in his head had faded, much like an old black-and-white negative.

He'd faced his fear and survived. This time. What about the next?

Chapter Five

Nicki gathered up her purse and satchel, slung them over her shoulder, then lifted Sadie into her arms. After turning out the lights in the office, she walked to the back door, surprised to find Ethan waiting. Normally she would resent anyone watching over her, but for some reason, she didn't mind. Maybe it was because of the robberies in town or maybe because he was so subtle about his concern. He smiled and pushed open the door. She expected him to offer to carry her bags, but he didn't. She appreciated that, too.

Outside she slipped the keys from her pocket and fumbled with them. Ethan took the keys from her hand, locked up, then handed them back.

"Most women I know could use an extra arm or two."

How did he know that? Had there been a lot of women in his life? "Thanks." She stepped off the stoop and walked toward her car, Ethan at her side. When she unlocked the door, he took the bags from her shoulder and placed them in the front seat while she settled Sadie in her car seat. "It's been a good day. Thanks for all your help."

Ethan nodded, stepping back as she climbed behind

the wheel. Before she could close the door, Ethan bent down to speak to her. He was so close she could see the small gold thread in his left iris and the thickness of his lashes.

"I've been thinking… I'd like to rent that one-bedroom apartment from you. The motel is getting cramped, and I've been meaning to look for a more permanent place. I think this would be a good option."

"But, Ethan, it's a mess."

He shrugged, one corner of his mouth lifting. "I could fix it up in the evenings. It won't take long. It might be a good idea to have someone on the premises, considering the thefts in town. Having lights on upstairs might make them think twice. Besides, it's really close to my work." He smiled.

Nicki smiled back. "I'll think about it."

"Fair enough. I'll see you tomorrow."

The next morning, on her way to work, she was still considering Ethan's suggestion. She wasn't sure it was a good idea. She knew practically nothing about him. For all she knew, he could be the thief robbing the stores. She shook off the ridiculous notion. Thanks to her mom and her late husband, she saw every man as a nefarious criminal.

From the backseat, Nicki heard Sadie fussing. She hadn't slept well last night and now Nicki was tired and irritable. Which was why she'd decided to go into the store early and start drawing up a new floor plan, or rather, adjusting the one she already had.

Lifting her daughter from the car seat, she unlocked the back door of Latimer's and stepped inside, suddenly aware of the eerie stillness inside the old building. A shudder chased down her spine. Most of the night she'd debated the wisdom of Ethan living above the store, but at the moment it felt like a great idea.

"What do you think, sweet pea? Should we rent an apartment to Ethan?" Sadie waved her hands. "Is that a yes?" Latimer's had little that anyone would want, but if she started selling electronics, that would change. Having Ethan upstairs would make her feel safer.

She cradled Sadie against her chest, closed the door and went into the office. "Having the rental income wouldn't hurt either, would it? But I don't think your grandma will like the idea." So maybe she wouldn't tell her.

After settling Sadie in her bouncy chair, Nicki pulled out her notes from the night before and went over her floor plan. The old computers qualified for the swap, which meant she'd be able to offer up-to-date electronics to their customers. Today she'd start brainstorming more ways to draw customers into the store. It had been years since she'd worked in the marketing business, and her skills were rusty, but with Ethan's help she might be able to turn things around before her dad came back to work. Plan A for the store might have fallen through, but plan A for her life—start a new life on her own— hadn't changed.

Unfortunately, when her attorney had called last night, she'd reported little progress in the negotiations toward a settlement with Brad's estate. Nicki knew she might never see any of that money, and without it, she was dependent on her parents. She needed a job, but applying now was pointless. Even if she received an offer, she wouldn't be able to accept it until her father was fully recovered. That meant for the next six to eight weeks, she was stuck.

"Good morning."

A smile moved her lips before she glanced up. There was no mistaking the deep, rich timbre that flowed through her like honey. Ethan leaned against the door frame, that crooked smile on his face. His jaw was shadowed with stubble, a look that suited him. The blue shirt he wore intensified his dark eyes, and the faded jeans hugged his strong legs, reminding her that his strength would be a blessing when they moved the fixtures. It also reminded her how comforting it was to have him on the premises. "Good morning."

"You're here early. Working on your plan B?"

"Yes, thanks to you. You've given me a whole new goal. I want to have everything finished in time for the Square Fair's sidewalk sale later this month. It'll be the perfect time to unveil the new look, and it's one of the most profitable days of the year."

Ethan's dark eyebrows arched. "Square Fair?"

"It's a whole day of events. The sidewalk sale is part of it. Square Fair started about ten years ago as a way to boost sales during the spring and raise money for local charities." Ethan frowned, crossing his arms over his chest and stretching the fabric of the blue shirt pleasingly across his muscled arms. "All the stores run specials that day and put merchandise on the sidewalk. There's a catfish cook-off in the courthouse park. The winner gets a cash prize and bragging rights for the year. Oh, and there's a concert that night, too. All the proceeds that day go to local charities. Mainly the battered women and homeless shelters."

"Sounds like a good cause."

Nicki looked away from his probing stare, tucking her hair behind her ears. She always had the feeling he was trying to figure her out. "I've been considering your offer to rent the apartment, and I think having you upstairs would be a good idea."

Ethan smiled. "Great. I'll get started fixing it up."

"You can move in as soon as you'd like. I suppose we should discuss the rent." She suggested an amount and Ethan quickly agreed. Nicki sighed in relief. She'd been afraid it was too high. Being able to count money coming in each month would give her some breathing room in her newly reduced budget. Having Ethan around greatly eased her fears. Especially since the burglars hadn't been caught yet. Once he moved in upstairs, she'd feel even more secure.

"Where would you like me to start today?"

"Would you look at this floor plan and tell me if it's possible using the old fixtures?" She'd intended to hand the paper to him, but he came to her side of the desk and leaned over her shoulder. He rested one hand on the back of her chair and placed the other on the desktop, fingers splayed as he looked at the plans.

He had nice hands, with long, tapered fingers, strong and capable. She fought the urge to look up at him. To do so would bring their faces close together, and her pulse was already racing from being so near his warm male energy.

He pointed to the area near the front door where she'd sketched a small rectangle. "What's this?"

"I thought it would be a good place to put that shelf that holds the day planners and date books."

Ethan picked up the drawings. "Let's go out front and take a look. I might be able to reconfigure one of the shelves to fit beside it."

Over the next half hour they came up with a plan that was both practical and economical. Nicki's confidence was soaring.

Back in the office Ethan glanced around the room. "Is the little one here today?"

Was he warming to her daughter? Nicki thought about that odd moment yesterday when she'd lifted Sadie from his arms. Their eyes had locked. The touch of his hand had jolted through her, connecting the three of them. Unable to explain it, she'd blamed it on fatigue and stress coupled with the nearness of a very compelling man with beautiful brown eyes.

"She's sleeping. Finally. She was up and down all night. I'd planned on working tonight, but I don't think I have the energy."

Ethan shifted his weight, slipping his hands into his back pockets. "I've been meaning to tell you. I can't work late on Wednesday nights."

"Oh. Church night, huh?"

His eyes held hers a moment, giving her the impression he was going to say something more.

"Right."

"No problem. I need to get back into church activities more, but I'm too tired these days. Maybe once things settle down." The excuse sounded false, even to her. The truth was, she didn't feel comfortable at Peace Community Church anymore, and she wasn't sure why. She'd grown up in that congregation, but each Sunday she found herself unable to concentrate and eager for the service to end. She'd even considered attending a different church.

As she went back to work, she wondered about Ethan's Wednesday night activities. She'd assumed he was going to church, but she had no reason to think that, other than he prayed before meals and he knew Jim Barrett. Her curiosity grew. She was coming to like Ethan, even trust him, but she knew little more about him now than she had a few days ago. What was he hiding? Or was he like her, merely keeping certain parts of his life private?

She kept her secrets out of shame. What secrets was he keeping?

Ethan had been back from lunch for barely a half hour when Sadie's loud cries sounded from the office. His heart raced as he hurried from the stockroom to the office in quick strides. He saw Nicki and the baby as she paced the small room, patting Sadie's little back and cooing softly.

"What's wrong with her? Is she all right?"

"She's tired. I'm hoping to get her settled down soon, but she won't eat. I think she might have an upset stomach." Nicki shifted the baby and lifted the bottle, touching it against the little mouth, but Sadie wasn't interested.

"What can you do?"

"Nothing. Just wait until she feels better. Ethan, do you think you could handle the sales counter for a half hour or so? If I can have a few more minutes with her, I think she'll calm down and eat. Then I can put her down for her nap."

Ethan tensed. "I'm not that experienced on the register yet." It was a lame excuse, but he wasn't looking forward to waiting on customers.

"You'll be fine. If you run into any difficulty, come and get me, but I don't think you'll have a problem."

He nodded, adding a reassuring smile he didn't feel. Nicki was struggling with the baby. The least he could do was wait on a few customers. Walking out into the store, he dragged a hand along the back of his neck, trying to ignore the nervousness in his chest. Stepping from behind the camera and dealing with people face-

to-face was still unnerving. Foster care had taught him strangers were people to be avoided. Not friends.

He stopped in the middle of the store, feeling exposed and vulnerable. Life was so much simpler when viewed through the camera lens. This was absurd. He'd spent three years in a war zone, but the thought of confronting customers left him jittery. Placing his hands on his hips, he scanned the store. Surely he could handle a few sales on his own.

He thought about Nicki and the way she approached each person who entered the store. She always smiled, always had a kind word for the customers, inquiring about them and their families. She flitted from one task to another, moving with so much energy and vitality he wondered where it all came from. Yet there were circles under her pretty eyes, and he'd seen the fatigue shadow her expression more times than he could count. She was doing a Herculean job of managing the store and caring for Sadie. He'd begun to worry that she'd collapse from sheer exhaustion. She'd mentioned that she lived with her parents and that her dad was recuperating from a kidney transplant. She needed help.

He was that help.

The doorbell jingled as he approached the sales counter. A middle-aged woman entered and walked straight to the back, turning down the middle aisle. He'd noticed that the customers knew exactly where to find what they were looking for. Not good. The first rule of retail was to keep the merchandise fresh by moving things around so customers would see something different each time they came.

"Excuse me."

He faced the customer, remembering to smile. "Yes, ma'am?"

She frowned. "Who are you?"

"Ethan Stone."

"You're the new guy Nichelle hired, right? I'm Sylvia Carver. My hubby, Aaron, and I own the furniture store across the way. Where did you hide those little dots?" She looked around.

"Ma'am?"

"I need those little colored sticky dots. I'm pricing items for the sidewalk sale and those are easy for people to see. And I need some of those little price tags with strings to attach to furniture pieces we'll put on the sidewalk."

Ethan led her to the aisle and pointed out the selection. She made her choice, then followed him to the checkout counter. "Y'all taking part in the sidewalk sale?"

"I believe so."

"Hello, Miss Sylvia." Nicki hurried forward and gave the woman a hug.

"Nice to see you, dear. How's that little girl of yours?"

"She's asleep. Finally." Nicki glanced at the items on the counter. "Did you find what you needed?"

"Thanks to your young man." She winked as she handed Ethan a credit card. "He tells me you're going to participate in the sidewalk sale this year. That's good to know. I talked to Angie Durrant, who's heading the Square Fair Committee, and she told me there are more stores signed up than ever before. Our little one-day event is becoming very popular."

"That's good to hear. We can use the extra sales."

"Can't we all." Sylvia picked up her package and left with a wave of her hand.

Nicki grabbed Ethan's forearm with both hands, a

big smile on her face. She looked like a little girl who'd been told she was going to see the circus.

"Did you hear what she said? The sale is going to be bigger than ever. We need to get busy around here. When can we start painting these shelves?"

Ethan chuckled. Her enthusiasm filled him with a desire to work round the clock to ensure her plan came together. "Who's this *we* you keep talking about? Does your hand fit a paintbrush?"

Nicki laughed and started back to the office, glancing over her shoulder at him with a teasing smile. "Yes, and a hammer and a saw. I'm very talented."

By the end of the day, Ethan had grown comfortable assisting customers, and Nicki had settled on the final arrangement for the shelves. It had been a good day and his relationship with Nicki had grown. Nicki's easygoing attitude and her welcoming spirit were giving him direction on how to live in the moment and not hide.

Ethan straightened up the stockroom before leaving at the end of the day. After a quick goodbye to Nicki, he got into his car and headed toward the Dixiana Motor Lodge. Tonight was his first meeting with Ron's PTSD group, and he didn't want to be late. After a quick stop at a fast-food place, he returned to his room. The place was really beginning to feel cramped. He was anxious to start fixing up the apartment above the store. Hopefully he'd have it ready by the weekend. He'd have to purchase furniture, a bed, dresser and a sofa. Maybe a flat-screen and kitchen items, but the old table and chairs in the place would suffice.

As he pulled his taco from the sack, his cell rang. A quick glance at the caller's name set his teeth on edge. Karen. His boss at TNZ. How had she found him?

He knew what she wanted. She wanted him back on a plane, headed to some foreign crisis, camera in hand. He'd told her repeatedly that he wasn't going back. His life as a photographer was over. But Karen refused to accept it. That was why he'd taken the leave of absence. He needed time to regroup, find out who he was and where he was going with his life.

Tossing the phone onto the bed, he decided that tomorrow he'd buy a new phone. Whatever it took to keep Karen Holt off his back.

Ethan had no trouble finding the church gym at Hope Chapel that evening. There was a noisy game of basketball going on when he entered. Ron Morrison came toward him with a welcoming smile. "Hey, Ethan. Glad you could make it." They shook hands. "Let me introduce you to the guys."

Ron was fifteen years older and a retired marine. Joe Ford, a stocky man of medium height, with intelligent eyes, was a former cop. Ethan guessed he was in his early forties. Stan Arnold was a retired career navy man. The other new member, Bobby Edmonds, was a twentysomething army corporal who'd been recently discharged.

Ethan knew each man had a story. He also knew from experience that it took time and trust before the members felt safe enough to open up and share their pain. He wasn't ready to reveal his experience tonight.

The aroma of fresh pizza brought shouts of approval from the men as a deliveryman walked into the gym with two large boxes. The smell triggered Ethan's hunger. He'd barely touched the taco after Karen's call.

Ron paid the man, then led the men to a small room off the gym filled with comfortable furniture and a table and chairs. After they'd quickly inhaled the pizza, Ron opened the meeting with prayer, then addressed upcoming service projects. "It's our week to work at the Dover homeless shelter. We'll be serving the meal from eleven to one on Sunday. I hope y'all will try and make it. Service projects are a key element in your recovery."

The new guy, Bobby, crossed his arms over his chest. "How's serving food going to help me with my PTSD?"

The man had a defiant tone to his voice. Ethan suspected Bobby was still at the stage where he felt his PTSD was a physical scar visible to everyone. Ethan remembered the feeling well and felt compelled to respond. He leaned forward, meeting Bobby's gaze. "Helping others takes your mind off your own problems and gives you a new perspective."

Ron nodded. "Ethan is right about that. It helps you see that everyone has problems."

Bobby shook his head. "Sounds too easy."

"It's not easy at all. But you won't know until you give it a shot."

After cleaning up the room, the men headed out. Ethan found himself walking to his car alongside Ron.

"So, you think you'll be able to help out at the shelter Sunday?"

Ethan had intended to skip it. He was eager to finish up the apartment over the store so he could move in after church. But then he thought about his reaction to seeing Nicki and Sadie and the moment in the park when he'd felt himself losing control. He needed this group, and he needed to be active. "Yeah, I think I am."

"Good. I'll see you there. If you want to ride together, let me know. And, Ethan, if you want to talk one-on-one, we can make time for that, too."

"Thanks." Ethan was always amazed at how God

worked in his life. First Paul and now Ron and the support group. The Lord always put people in his path to help him along the next step. What he couldn't figure out was why Nicki and the baby were in his life. What possible good could come from having the constant reminder of his trauma in front of him every day? He was handling it so far, but he'd have to be vigilant. All he could do was walk by faith and not sight because seeing them every day would be like juggling a time bomb.

Ethan slid his arm into the sleeve of his plaid shirt, wincing when the muscles in his shoulders and back protested. He'd spent most of yesterday dismantling the old store shelves. He should have rested last night, but he was determined to finish the apartment before Sunday so he could get settled in. After a quick sandwich at the Magnolia Café, he'd spent the evening cleaning and making minor repairs on the plumbing and electric. It had been nearly one in the morning when he'd stopped, so he'd spent another night in his sleeping bag. Thankfully he'd packed a change of clothes and a few other necessities into the car, along with his well-traveled coffeemaker.

Walking into the bathroom, he leaned toward the mirror, gently removing the tiny piece of tissue he'd placed over the nick on his jaw he'd made while shaving. He should have left the stubble, but he'd decided to adopt a more professional appearance.

Be honest, Stone. He sighed and stared at his reflection. He wanted to look good for Nicki. Trouble was, he didn't know why. Foster care had taught him early how to keep himself detached from his emotions and maintain a safe distance in his relationships. But it had cost him.

The one woman he'd loved had ended their engagement, calling him cold, empty and incapable of living a normal life. LeAnn had accused him of hiding behind his camera to avoid living in the real world. He'd been unable to disagree with her. He'd loved her, but he hadn't known how to let her into his heart. He'd never cared for anyone since.

What would that woman say if she could see him now? The explosion and the horrific picture had changed him forever, and not only physically, with the scars on his face and arm. He'd awoken in the army hospital drowning in a flood of feelings he couldn't control and had spent the past year learning to manage his emotions without shutting them down completely.

But Nicki was different. She was a fountain of emotion. She wore each one with ease, moving from happy to irritated to sad in an instant, leaving him to marvel at her adaptability. Watching her expressive face and gestures had become his favorite form of entertainment.

But he had questions. She'd given him his first paycheck last night, signed with her married name, Collier. Yet she went by her maiden name and she didn't wear a ring, and he couldn't forget the way she'd bluntly said her husband was dead, displaying no emotion at all.

She was running from something. Sometimes he could see the longing to leave Dover in her eyes, and it left him with burrs in his heart. He wasn't ready to see another person he cared for walk away.

Ethan glanced at his watch. He was anxious to get back to work on the fixtures. Weather permitting, he'd start painting the shelves today. Stepping to one of the two small windows in the back of the apartment, he looked down at the parking area just as Nicki's car pulled into view. He watched as she removed the baby from the car seat, holding her tenderly and placing a kiss on her cheek. He smiled, realizing he was enjoying the sight of them together instead of bracing against a possible emotional attack.

Perhaps his exposure to the mother and child would be a good thing. He had to admit he looked forward to coming to work each day and he suspected the engaging Nicki was the reason.

Nicki made a sweep of the aisles, straightening up and checking for bins and shelves low on merchandise. The quiet gave her a moment to regroup and remember that she wasn't truly alone in her situation. She had Sadie. Though she'd greatly underestimated the time and energy required to manage the store and care for a baby. She'd stolen a few minutes this morning for devotional time, reading her favorite verses, but they hadn't provided the usual comfort. She'd blamed it on fatigue and being overwhelmed by problems at the store.

She'd been surprised to see Ethan's car already parked behind the store when she arrived this morning. He'd appeared at the top of the back stairs and hurried down to help carry Sadie's things inside. He'd explained that he'd worked on the apartment and had slept there last night.

Now he was eager to start rearranging the fixtures. His eagerness to work was admirable. Perhaps she should give him a key to the store. That way when he was ready to work, he wouldn't have to wait for her to show up. Wouldn't her mother love that idea? A stranger with access to the entire building.

She caught sight of Ethan as he walked from the kitchen to the stockroom. She'd tried not to notice the way he looked today. His face was clean shaven, revealing the interesting little scar above his mouth and the deep planes of his cheeks. The pale green shirt made his dark good looks even harder to ignore. In a few short days he'd become more than an employee and more like a friend.

The morning passed quickly. Sadie took a long nap, which gave Nicki time to rearrange the merchandise and clear more fixtures for painting. Ethan had already finished several. The store was in a state of upheaval, but hopefully for only a few days. Her excitement grew as she saw her new plan coming to life. She hoped her father would approve. More important, she hoped her plan worked.

Nicki glanced up as the doorbell jingled, smiling when she saw Shelby Durrant and her stepdaughter, Cassidy, enter. "Good afternoon. How's the scrapbooking store coming, Shelby?"

"We'll be open in time for the sidewalk sale. How about you? I hear Latimer's is getting a makeover." She scanned the store. "Wow. You *are* making changes."

"I couldn't have done it without Ethan's help. Can I help you find something? Most of our merchandise is still on the floor, but it's been shuffled around."

Shelby glanced down at Cassidy, giving her an encouraging nod.

"I got my first cell phone for my birthday, and Miss Debi told me you have some really cool covers."

Nicki blinked, darting a questioning glance at Shelby. "I just put them out yesterday. How did you know?"

"We saw Debi at soccer practice last night."

That explained it. Debi was almost as excited about the new merchandise as Nicki. "They're over by the front window." Cassidy exclaimed in delight over the selection of covers. Everything from faux diamonds, sequins, geometric patterns and textured designs.

"I want them all. I don't know how I'll choose just one. These are awesome."

The girl's enthusiasm gave Nicki an idea, and she walked over to the display. "Cassidy, how would you like to have one free of charge?" The girl stared wide-eyed. "But I need a favor in return. I'll give you the cover of your choice, but I want you to tell all your friends where you got it and encourage them to come and buy them from me. How's that sound?"

Cassidy nodded eagerly. "I can do that."

"Is it all right with you, Shelby? I think it would help bring customers in if they see we're carrying new things now."

"I don't see a problem, and I know what you mean about bringing in customers. My brother-in-law Adam is making changes since he took over the hardware store. His ideas are really helping."

"Are your in-laws ready to retire?"

"They were, but now they're not so sure. With new grandchildren on the horizon, they might hang around a bit longer." She rested her hand across the bump in her belly.

"Grand*children*?"

"Ty and Ginger are expecting, too. They just told us last night."

"That was quick."

"They were surprised, but excited."

Shelby had married Matt Durrant last fall. Matt's sister, Laura, had recently married, and her husband was now running Durrant's Hardware. Their brother Ty had married this past Valentine's Day. The thought of all those happy couples left Nicki with a hollow sensation in her chest. She'd like to have someone special in her life, but after what she'd been through, she was content for now with her sweet Sadie.

Cassidy chose a bright pink cell-phone cover overlaid with clear bugle beads. Nicki watched the pair leave together, giggling with joy. Someday, she and Sadie would be doing mother-and-daughter things. She couldn't wait.

Ethan walked toward her, setting off a little flutter in her heart. She looked away. He was a nice man. Solid. Dependable. Reliable. All those qualities she'd look for next time. But she needed to get her life back on track before she thought about another relationship. Especially with a guy who was secretive about his background. Still, she had a feeling Ethan would be a good dad. A man like her father.

Shaken by the thought, she went into her office and closed the door. Her instincts were telling her Ethan was a good man, but there was another voice whispering in her head, reminding her of her poor judgment with men. Which voice did she listen to?

Maybe the answer was neither. She would focus on saving Latimer's and not her growing awareness of Ethan. She had a feeling that would be easier said than done.

Chapter Six

Nicki heard the sound of the back door squeaking open later that afternoon, but kept her focus on the papers in front of her. It was probably Ethan going outside again. She'd noticed he'd step outside now and then. He wouldn't be gone long and she was curious what he did out there. She knew he didn't smoke; maybe he needed fresh air. The stockroom could get stuffy with the dust from the boxes and packing material.

"Nichelle?"

Nicki froze. Her mom. Great. Ethan had already removed several of the shelving units and the store was a mess. "In here."

Her mother walked into the office, scanning the room. "Where's Sadie?"

Nicki nodded toward the other room, where the baby was entertaining herself in her bouncy chair surrounded by colorful movable toys. Her mother went to the child and bent over, speaking quietly to her granddaughter.

"She shouldn't be here. It's not good for her. She should be at the house."

"Mom, she's perfectly all right. You have enough on your hands with Dad recuperating."

"Your father is doing fine. He'll be back to work in no time." Her mother glanced over her shoulder. "What are you working on there?"

Nicki clicked off the computer monitor and stood. She had no intention of telling her mother how bad things were. "The usual paperwork. What are you doing here?"

"I had a prescription to pick up for your father, and I thought I'd stop in to check on things."

Dread pulled Nicki's mood down a few notches. "Check on things" was her mom's code for "make sure things were done her way."

"Things are fine, Mom. I've got it under control."

"I'm sure you do, but I haven't been in the store in ages. I'd like to tell your father how things are going." She walked out of the office, forcing Nicki to follow.

Bracing herself for an argument, Nicki watched as her mother made a sweep of the store. She knew the moment her mother's fuse lit. She stopped at the tables in the front filled with school merchandise and other outdated items Nicki was determined to unload.

Her mother pointed to the bins. "What is this? Why are you discounting all these supplies? You should be holding them for the back-to-school rush at the end of summer."

"Mom, we need to get rid of this stuff and bring in notebooks and supplies that will appeal more to the kids." She wanted to tell her mom that the sale was actually doing quite well, but her self-confidence abruptly sagged. She'd never had trouble standing up to her mother before, but since coming home, she'd suffered unexpected moments of insecurity.

Her mother set her lips in a firm line and gestured to the open floor space where Ethan had removed a section of shelving. "And what's going on here? Where are the fixtures? Where have you moved the paper clips and staplers? Customers expect to find them right here."

"Mom, I'm rearranging the floor. It's time to freshen things up. It's been laid out like this for decades."

"That's because it works, and customers like it that way." She gestured to the sale table. "You'll never sell these items this way. It looks like a cheap discount store, putting things in plastic bins. Honestly, Nichelle, what were you thinking?"

Maybe her mom was right. Maybe her plan wasn't a good one. She'd worked in marketing only a few years before Brad had convinced her to quit. She wasn't an expert. What made her think that she could magically turn the business around?

"Excuse me."

Ethan's deep voice was a welcome intrusion. She turned and saw him carrying a large carton of spiral notebooks toward the front. He gave Nicki a knowing and sympathetic grin.

"I noticed the bins were getting low."

Her mother pierced him with a fierce glare. "You're the man my daughter hired?"

Ethan set the box on the table and began transferring the notebooks to the bin. "Yes, ma'am." He faced her, but didn't extend his hand.

Nicki sighed in relief. Good move. Her mother would have ignored it anyway.

"I want you to know I was opposed to the idea. We don't know anything about you."

"Mother, please."

"I'll tell you straight up, young man. If you so much as take a pencil, an eraser or a piece of paper that doesn't belong to you, I will notify the authorities."

"I understand. You have nothing to worry about."

Her mother continued to glare. Ethan continued to fill up the bins. Her mother watched a moment, then stepped forward.

"When did you start this sale?"

Nicki sighed. "A few days ago."

"You've sold a bin's worth already?"

"More than that," Ethan replied promptly. "I've filled these bins up at least twice a day." Ethan finished his task, then faced her mother. "Nice to meet you, Mrs. Latimer." With a nod, he walked away, leaving Nicki with an overwhelming sense of gratitude and an irrational impulse to hug him.

Her mother studied the bins a moment, then faced her. "You know you'll have to replace all that merchandise before the school rush starts."

"I know. Don't worry."

Her mother huffed in irritation before starting back to the office. "How can you hear Sadie when she cries if you're way out here?"

"I have a monitor out here under the counter. I hear every noise she makes."

"I certainly hope so. I don't want her ignored for a customer."

"She won't be."

Her mother nodded then placed a quick kiss on Nicki's cheek. "I'll see you this evening."

After her mother left, Nicki sagged behind the sales counter. No matter what she did, it would never be right. She could only pray that her father would keep her mother occupied and that her plan for invigorating business would work.

She straightened to see Ethan coming toward her, an expression of disbelief on his face.

"Your mother is a woman of strong opinions."

"That's putting it mildly. She and I are like oil and water. My brother was her favorite. He could do no wrong. I could do nothing right. Thank you for stepping in."

"Don't worry about it. I was only telling the truth. The sale has gone well. It was a good idea." He leaned down, tapping the back of her hand lightly with his fingers. "Don't let anyone make you doubt your decisions. You know what you're doing."

His confidence in her filled her with a warm glow. It *had* been a good decision. "Thank you, but that's easier said than done."

He nodded, his expression turning serious. "Once your belief in yourself is shattered, it's hard to rebuild it."

"Is that even possible?" There were days when her lack of confidence weighed on her so heavily it was hard to take the next step.

"With prayer and a lot of determination." He smiled then retreated to the stockroom.

Nicki watched him go, wondering what had shattered his belief in himself. He'd spoken with conviction and she'd seen that distant look that she'd seen before someplace, but couldn't remember. Something awful had happened to him. Maybe that was what she'd sensed in him the day they'd met. Both had suffered events that had changed them.

Ethan was right about one thing. She would need prayer and determination to face the challenges ahead and she had an abundance of both.

Saturday morning Nicki sat at her desk marveling at how quickly her life had gotten complicated. Ethan had just informed her that he was having his new furniture delivered to his apartment this afternoon, which meant he'd be living over the store from now on, and she hadn't told her folks yet. Having a tenant wasn't going to go down well with her mom, but she didn't have the strength to battle with her today. If only she had someone to help her break the news. Ethan. Of course. It was the perfect solution.

She had been looking for a way to thank him for backing her up with her mom yesterday. She knew he ate out all the time, so he was probably ready for a home-cooked meal. If Ethan was with her when she dropped her bomb, her mother couldn't explode. She might have been rude to him as an employee, but she would never be rude in front of a guest. By the time Ethan left, her mom would be calm enough to see reason.

She winced inwardly as she realized her idea would put Ethan in an awkward position again. But he was a big boy. And a gentleman. He could deal.

Pushing away from her desk, she hurried to the stockroom, but it was empty. She checked the sales floor. No Ethan and, sadly, no customers. She headed for the back door and found him standing in the parking area staring upward, hands shoved into his back pockets. Something about the set of his shoulders suggested he was praying. She paused, waiting for some sign he was finished. He must have sensed her presence, for he lowered his head and slowly glanced over his shoulder. His eyes were shadowed for a moment. Then they cleared and his mouth moved upward on one side. "You looking for me?"

"Yes. I have an invitation for you." He turned and came toward her.

"What kind of invitation?"

"Dinner. At my parents'. Tonight." The puzzled look

in his brown eyes made her question her plan. Ethan wasn't a talkative man. He seemed most content when he was alone. Tossing him into the middle of her family was a horrible idea.

"Why?"

His one-word response confirmed her doubts, but she couldn't handle her mother alone. "Well, Mom's fixing her special pork roast tonight, and I've noticed you always eat out and I thought you might be ready for a home-cooked meal." She kept her smile in place, mentally crossing her fingers.

"All right. When and where?"

"Oh, uh, you can just ride with me. We'll go right after work, and then I'll bring you back here." He'd been camping out in the apartment the past couple of nights while he fixed things up.

He eyed her curiously for a moment, then nodded. "Okay. Thanks."

"Well, I'll leave you to your break." She backed up, then hurried toward the stoop outside the back entrance, but as she reached for the door handle, Ethan's strong arm grasped it first and pulled it open. He had his sleeves rolled up past his elbows and she saw a long red scar across his left forearm. She wanted to ask him about it, but lacked the courage.

"Break's over."

She looked up at him. Trapped between him and the door, she couldn't ignore him or his woodsy scent. Her attraction to Ethan was becoming troublesome. Suddenly the invitation to her parents' home felt like a very bad idea.

Ethan maneuvered the passenger seat in Nicki's small compact as far back as the baby seat behind him would permit to give himself more leg room. He'd suspected her invitation to have dinner with her folks was more for her benefit than his own. After meeting her mother the other day, he figured the family meal might not be that warm and cozy. If she needed a diversion, he didn't mind playing the part. And she was right about one thing. He was tired of eating out. Once he settled in the upstairs apartment, he'd brush up his mediocre cooking skills.

He turned his attention to Nicki, who clutched the steering wheel in a death grip while she chatted nervously about random topics as they drove.

"So anyway, when the town started to rebuild, they wanted to do a better job, so they called the town Do Over, but over time the name morphed into Dover. I know for a while they spelled it D'Over, with the apostrophe, but now it's just Dover. A few people here are trying to get it changed back to preserve the town's history, but I don't know if that'll fly or not."

Ethan tried to hide his grin. Life with Nicki would never be dull. Even when she was trying to hide her nervousness by babbling, she was fascinating. A living prism refracting her emotions in every direction without fear. He envied her that ability. Paul had told him emotions wouldn't kill him; it only felt as if they would. Maybe she could teach him.

Nicki slowed the car, pulling into the drive of a charming Tudor-style home with a neatly trimmed yard and colorful flower beds. Parking the car in front of the garage, she sighed and glanced at him with a tight smile.

"Here we are. Hope you're hungry. Mom loves to cook."

"Good to hear."

Ethan helped her get Sadie out of the car seat and carried the diaper bag. As they approached the front door, he tensed, uncertain of the reception he'd receive. Her mother hadn't been too pleased with his being hired.

"Mom, we're here." Nicki led him into a large cheery kitchen. The decor was warm and welcoming. He hoped her mother would be the same. Mrs. Latimer was at the stove. She smiled at him, but he sensed she wasn't too happy about having him as a guest.

"Good to see you again, Mrs. Latimer."

"Mr. Stone." She turned back to the stove. "We're almost ready. Go clean up."

"Where's Daddy?"

Ethan smiled at Nicki's use of the childhood term. She must be close to her father.

"Right here, pumpkin."

The distinguished gentleman came slowly into the kitchen. He looked good for someone who'd had a kidney transplant only a short time ago.

"This must be our new employee. I'm Allen Latimer."

Ethan shook his hand. It was strong and firm, and he sensed an energy about the man that echoed his daughter's. "Yes, sir."

Mr. Latimer lifted the baby into his arms, cuddling her close. "Nichelle, why don't you bring Sadie's swing into the dining room so she can sit with us while we eat."

Ethan glanced at Nicki. "I'll get it. Just tell me where it is."

"I'll show you."

Ethan followed Nicki through the house into a room crammed with a double bed, boxes and a crib and changing table. It had to be difficult to relax in a place like this. She obviously needed more room. And some privacy. Picking up the baby swing, he started back through the house, contemplating an idea.

The family settled into the dining room, as Nicki showed Ethan where to place the swing. Her father slipped Sadie into the seat, fastened the strap and set the swing in motion. Nicki took the chair beside Sadie, and Ethan chose the one next to Nicki. He decided to let Nicki do most of the talking. He didn't want to stir up any more trouble for Nicki with her mother.

"So I'm guessing you're a military man." Allen Latimer smiled across the table. "I served four years in the army. Best experience of my life. What branch were you with?"

Ethan froze, his hand grasping his water glass. How did he answer that question? He didn't want to start a discussion that might be unpleasant for his hosts. He could sense all three Latimers waiting for his answer. Inhaling a deep breath, he said, "I'm sorry to say I never had the honor of serving in the armed forces, sir."

Allen frowned, his eyes probing. "You don't say. I could have sworn you had a military air about you. I'm never wrong." Then his gaze lightened, and he leaned back. "Well, guess there's always a first time. Must be all this medication I'm on. Our son was a marine. We lost him two years ago."

Ethan stole a quick look at Nicki, who had her head lowered. Why hadn't she told him? "I'm sorry to hear that." An awkward silence settled over the room before Nicki's dad spoke again.

"So where are you staying, Mr. Stone?"

"For the moment I'm at the Dixiana."

"Flora Edwards runs a nice place."

"Yes, sir, she does." Ethan tensed, uncomfortable

with the shallow conversation meant to bridge the gap between remembered grief and normalcy.

Mr. Latimer lowered his chin and eyed him closely. "You said 'for the moment.' Are you moving?"

Ethan glanced at Nicki. Hadn't she told them about the apartment?

"Mom, Ethan has fixed up the small apartment upstairs from the store. He's going to be staying there from now on."

Ethan didn't have to look at Mrs. Latimer to know she was unhappy.

"When did this happen?" Her tone was thick with displeasure.

"His furniture was delivered this afternoon. Mom, it's a good idea. He'll be paying rent, and having someone on the premises 24/7 will provide security for the store. I know I'll feel safer when I come in each morning, and if I have to work late I won't have to worry that I might be putting Sadie at risk."

"A security system would do the same thing."

Allen smiled over at his wife. "But a security system costs money, Myra, which is why we haven't done it before. This way, Ethan is paying us. With all the robberies going on downtown, I think it sounds like a good solution."

"We'll see about that."

Myra Latimer stood and picked up her and her husband's plate. "I'm sure everyone is ready for dessert. Nichelle, I could use your help."

Ethan gave Nicki an encouraging smile. He suspected a one-sided mother-daughter discussion was going to take place in the kitchen. And from the expression on Mr. Latimer's face, he suspected it, too. They shared a knowing grin.

"I didn't mean to cause a problem."

Mr. Latimer waved off his concern. "I think it was a good idea. My wife and daughter are often on opposing sides."

"I've noticed." Glancing over his shoulder, Ethan made sure the women were still in the other room. Now might be a good time to mention the idea he'd had. "Sir, I was wondering if I could ask you something."

Mr. Latimer smiled and nodded. "Ask away."

"I'd like your permission to fix up the other apartment above your store for Nicki and the baby to use." He watched the older man for some sign of approval. "She works hard all day, running the store and caring for Sadie. I thought it might be good for her to have a place of her own. Somewhere to unwind without having—" He searched for words that wouldn't offend.

"Without having to deal with her mother or her father?"

"No, sir, I didn't mean that."

"Son, I'm not unaware of the tension between my wife and daughter. I've made a mess of things over the last few years. Now it's up to my daughter to fix it. Nicki is trying hard to not add more stress to this family. I think fixing that apartment for her and the baby is a great idea. Go for it. You have my stamp of approval."

Ethan met the other man's eyes. "Thank you. I think it'll make things easier for her."

"What all do you plan on doing?"

"Mainly clean the place up. Paint. Do a few repairs. Take down wallpaper."

"The floors up there are wood beneath that carpet. Should look pretty good after a thorough cleaning. Wish I could lend you a hand, but I'm afraid I'm in no shape to help right now."

"No problem. My evenings are free. And I like the work."

Nicki and her mother returned with plates of pecan pie and ice cream. Ethan's mouth watered, and his heart felt lighter. He'd had a home-cooked meal and gained Mr. Latimer's approval on the other apartment. It had been a good day. He was anxious to get started.

Anger had Nicki gripping the steering wheel of her car with white-knuckled force as she drove back to the store. She'd been worried about how her parents would take to Ethan, and instead she'd found herself furious with him.

"Why did you lie to my father?"

"I didn't."

Nicki darted a glance in his direction. The deep frown creasing his forehead showed his confusion. "Really? I know you were hiding something. I saw a look in your eyes that I've seen before. Then tonight when Dad asked if you had served in the military, I realized I'd seen that same look in my brother's eyes. You *were* in the military. What happened? Were you booted out?"

Ethan shook his head. "No. I was telling the truth. I was never in the armed forces. But…I was in Afghanistan for three years."

"Doing what?"

"Working for a private firm."

Nicki was positive he was telling her only part of it. "So why didn't you just say so?"

"Telling war stories over the dinner table isn't exactly great conversation. Especially considering your brother died over there."

Nicki couldn't argue with him there. "So is that why

you left out past employment details on your application?"

"Is that what has you upset?" He frowned in disbelief. "I took a leave from my job to see what direction my life would take going forward. Dover seemed like a nice place to reassess. That's all."

She wanted to believe him. "I don't like being misled. Or manipulated."

"But you don't mind manipulating other people."

She jerked her head to look at him. "What do you mean?" The knowing glint in his eyes told her she'd been caught. One corner of his mouth lifted, sending a rush of heat into her cheeks.

"I know you asked me to dinner so I could be your deflector when you told your mother I was moving into the apartment."

"Ethan, I—" There was no way she could explain. He was right.

"It's okay. I get it. And I don't mind being your buffer. And I really did need a good home-cooked meal."

Her conscience pressed her to give an explanation. She pulled the car to a stop near the stairs at the back of the store. "Okay, you're right about me using you to soften my mother's reaction. I'm sorry. As for the other, my ex was very secretive and manipulating, and he—"

Ethan touched her arm. He held her gaze with his penetrating dark eyes, and she had the odd feeling he understood more than she'd intended him to.

"You don't need to tell me. We both have things in our pasts we're not ready to share. Give it time."

He reached for the door handle. "I will tell you I'm not a criminal on the run or a celebrity hiding out. Just a guy looking for a fresh start." The humor in his tone made her smile.

"Fair enough."

He winked, causing her heart to skip a beat. "See you Monday morning."

"Are you going back to the Dixiana, or are you spending the night here?" A rush of embarrassment warmed her cheeks, making her glad it was dark in the car. For some reason, she wasn't ready for him to go.

"I have my furniture now, so I'll probably stay here tonight, then pick up the rest of my things from the motel tomorrow after church."

"Do you need any help?" What was wrong with her? She spent enough time with Ethan. She didn't need to spend any more. That would be playing with fire.

"Are you offering?"

"You've helped me. That's what friends do."

"Friends. Of course. Thanks, but I don't have much to move. I do have several things to assemble. How are you with an Allen wrench?"

"Allen who?"

He chuckled and reached over to squeeze her hand. "I appreciate the offer. You're very sweet. But you have enough on your plate without worrying about me. I'll see you on Monday." He climbed out of the car and started up the outside steps.

Nicki waited until he disappeared behind the steel door before starting her car and heading home. Thoughts of Ethan dominated her thoughts far into the night. No matter how hard she tried to stop them.

Chapter Seven

Sunday afternoon blossomed into the perfect spring day. Nicki had taken Sadie for a stroll around her parents' neighborhood, enjoying the flowers and the warm sunshine. The fresh air had renewed her spirits and given her a brief escape from the confines of the store. It had also given her an idea that she was beginning to regret.

Pulling her car to a stop beside Ethan's behind the store, she questioned the wisdom of showing up unannounced. She wasn't sure what wild hair had taken hold of her to bring Ethan a hot meal today. Maybe it was the obvious delight he'd shown over her mother's dinner last night. Or maybe it was her Southern upbringing, which dictated a new neighbor required a welcome meal.

Lifting the food carrier from the backseat, she glanced up at the door at the top of the outside stairs. She would simply drop off the food and leave.

As she climbed the stairs, she had to face the truth. The food was a means of showing Ethan her appreciation for all he'd done. In less than a week he'd renewed her hope and strengthened her confidence. That deserved an acknowledgment. It was a tiny gesture, but she didn't know what else to do.

At the top of the stairs Nicki unlocked the outside door and stepped into the hall. Her nerves quickened. What if he didn't like jambalaya? She shook her head and strode toward his apartment door. It didn't matter. It was the gesture that counted. She'd hand him the food then go. No big deal. But as she neared Ethan's door, her heartbeat quickened. Why was she so nervous? Taking a fortifying breath, she knocked firmly on the door.

He opened the door, his expression shifting quickly from surprise to a warm smile. "Hey. What are you doing here?"

Nicki took a moment to appreciate her employee. He looked incredibly handsome and all male in worn jeans and a white T-shirt that emphasized his broad chest. Quickly shoving her thoughts aside, she held out the covered dish. "I brought you something to eat. I figured you'd be too busy moving in so..." She shrugged, suddenly at a loss for words.

"Wow. Thanks." He stepped aside. "Come on in."

She moved into the small space beside the efficiency kitchen and set the dish on the old battered table, which, along with the chairs, had been given a fresh coat of white paint.

Ethan leaned over the container. "This smells amazing."

Nicki smiled. "I hope you like andouille jambalaya."

"I do. Did your mom make this?"

"No." She feigned insult. "I did. I'll have you know I'm a very good cook."

Ethan smiled. "Then I know I'll love it."

The warmth in his tone pleased her more than it should have. She surveyed the small apartment to regain her composure. "I can't believe this is the same place." The walls had been painted a soothing beige; a comfy sofa and recliner were in the living area. A large flat-screen TV with wires and a cable dangling from the side sat at an angle on a small console. The efficiency kitchen was clean and sparkling. At the other end, she glimpsed the bedroom and a new chest of drawers. "I never thought this place could look so good."

"All it needed was a little love and attention. It'd been neglected for a long time."

Nicki glanced over her shoulder, her gaze landing on his. There was quiet understanding in his brown eyes that told her he wasn't talking only about the apartment. Ethan had an unsettling ability to look beyond her facade and sense her real feelings.

"Uh, well, enjoy the meal. I'll pick the dish up later."

He reached out and took her arm before she could turn around. "Whoa. Aren't you going to stay and eat with me? I don't want to eat alone."

The moment he made the offer, she realized that was what she'd been hoping he'd say. "Well, I suppose I could. I haven't eaten yet."

"Great. I'll get the plates." Ethan went into the kitchen while Nicki cleared the table and removed the lid from the carrier. The tantalizing aroma of spicy jambalaya and corn bread filled the room.

Ethan returned with the paper plates, plastic utensils and a sheepish look. "All I have." He inhaled, closing his eyes. "Wow. That smells amazing."

Nicki filled their plates, adding large pieces of corn bread on the side. Ethan wasted no time sampling the food. "Oh. Wow. Can you cook for me every night?"

Nicki froze with her fork halfway to her mouth. She knew what he meant. But the image that called up in her mind was something else entirely. A normal life, someone waiting for her at the end of the day. Someone who truly cared about her and what she wanted. She shook off the thought.

"Nope. That wasn't part of the rental agreement."

He chuckled, the sound of it skittering inside her heart. "Where's Sadie?"

"With my mom, but I really don't like to ask her to babysit."

Ethan frowned. "She's a new grandma. I'd think she'd love that."

"Oh, she does, but she has enough on her mind with my dad. I've already complicated things by coming home without warning and adding a baby to their lives. Besides, Sadie is my responsibility. I can take care of us without any help."

"I have no doubt."

"I only left her with them this time because Sadie is asleep, so she won't be any trouble for them." She knew he saw the lie for what it was. She'd wanted to see him.

Ethan speared a piece of andouille sausage and broke his plastic fork in half. His expression was so priceless, Nicki burst out laughing. "You need to invest in some real silverware. Not to mention plates."

"Hey, they're on my shopping list." He reached for a piece of paper and handed it to her. "See. Right there. Dishes, spoons, knives and forks."

Nicki took the list and scanned it. "You need to add a few things. Like a broom and dustpan. A can opener. Don't forget dish soap and a toaster." The more she thought about what he'd need, the more excited she became. She missed having a home of her own to furnish. "Do you have a toilet-bowl brush?"

Ethan laughed out loud. His dark eyes were warm and sparkling. "I want to go shopping right now."

She giggled. "I'm just trying to think of all the things a man wouldn't think to buy."

He placed his hand over hers, curling his thumb up into her palm.

"Maybe you should come with me when I go to the store. As my personal shopper."

She liked the idea of helping him pick out things he needed. Then reality kicked in. It was time to go.

"Sadie will be waking soon. I'd better get back." She stood, tucking her hair behind her ear, suddenly nervous around Ethan. He made her think about a different future, but she couldn't afford to get tangled up again. "I'll pick up the baking dish later."

"I'll walk you out."

"You don't need to."

He smiled into her eyes. "I know, but I want to. Those steps are steep and narrow. The furniture deliverymen never failed to point that out on each trip up here."

The feel of his hand in the center of her back as they walked out onto the landing gave her a sense of comfort and security. She didn't want to be protected— she'd had too much of that from her late husband. But Ethan's protectiveness didn't make her feel stifled; it made her feel safe.

At her car, Ethan opened the door for her. "Thanks again for the meal. That was sweet of you. It's been a long time since someone thought about me that way."

"We're friends. Friends think about each other."

"Yes. They do." He reached out and gently brushed back a strand of hair that the breeze had dislodged. "I'll see you tomorrow."

Nicki climbed in her car and pulled out into the alley,

but when she glanced in her rearview mirror, she smiled. Ethan was still standing there, watching her drive away.

Latimer's Office Supply was open and ready for business. It was also devoid of customers. Ethan had opened the store twenty minutes ago, but not one person had come through the door. Granted, it was early on a Tuesday, but normally someone from one of the nearby businesses would come in needing some small item, and they usually took a moment to ask about Sadie or chat with Nicki.

But she wasn't here. Nicki had taken Sadie for a pediatrician checkup and had left him in charge of the store for a few hours. He'd grown comfortable helping the customers and no longer wanted to hide in the stockroom. But the quiet now gave him too much time to think about Nicki and her reasons for bringing him the jambalaya. He wanted to believe it was more than just a friendly gesture, that it meant she thought about him after work hours. Mostly he wanted to believe she enjoyed spending time with him.

Nicki was the first woman in a very long time that made him think about a future. Her bright smile and her boundless energy were like a sweet infusion of adrenaline each time he was near her. But she didn't seem ready for any kind of relationship. Her focus right now was on saving the store. His was on finding a new direction for his life. Which was why a few customers would be nice. To keep such thoughts at bay.

As if reading his thoughts, two gentlemen entered the store, glanced at him briefly and moved on to walk through the aisles, not giving him a chance to offer his assistance. A few moments later, the taller man stepped from the third aisle. "Where did you hide the computer paper?"

Ethan pointed toward the next row of shelves. "It's right around the corner."

The man frowned and glanced around. "Moving things around, huh?"

"We're doing a little reorganizing, yes, sir." The man nodded and went in search of the paper.

The men's voices could be heard as they walked the aisles. Ethan ignored them until he heard them mention the robberies.

"...another one last night. This is getting out of hand. Why can't the police department catch these bozos?"

The tall man appeared from the center aisle. "Beats me." He placed his items on the counter. Two reams of paper, a pack of high-quality pens, a roll of tape and box of staples.

Ethan hadn't heard about any new robberies, but he was more convinced than ever that taking the apartment upstairs was a wise move. He rang up the sale, bagged it and thanked them. The other man slid his purchases toward him, pulling out his debit card.

"If you ask me, it's probably some crazed ex-soldier looking for drug money. Why else would he be hitting the downtown stores?"

The tall man laughed. "No kidding. There're all a bunch of PTSD wackos."

Ethan clenched his jaw. Thanks to movies and TV shows, most people now thought PTSD sufferers were ticking time bombs poised to turn into homicidal maniacs. He resisted the impulse to set the men straight, knowing that antagonizing Nicki's few customers wouldn't help her business. But the comments did reinforce his decision to not tell Nicki about his emotional problems.

"We're back."

The sound of Nicki's voice flowed through him like warm sunshine. He breathed a sigh of relief when he saw the big smile on her face. But as she approached with Sadie, a new vision flashed through his mind. The mother and child in Afghanistan were walking in a market. He sucked in a breath, forcing the image back into the recesses of his mind. This was Nicki and Sadie. The others were gone. He turned aside briefly to collect himself before forcing a smile and facing them. All he saw was a lovely smiling mom with her sweet little girl.

He reached out for Sadie when they drew close, settling her on his shoulder. She tilted her head to look at him, grabbing his lower lip with tiny fingers.

"How is she? No problems?"

Nicki gently stroked the tiny arm. "Not a one. She's right on track for everything. The doctor said she's very strong for her age." Nicki smiled at him. "How about here? Any problems?"

Ethan handed the baby back to her. "Nothing I couldn't handle."

Ethan watched them walk away, a strange sensation blooming inside his chest. What would it be like to take care of Nicki and Sadie? To make sure they were safe and happy? He'd like to try, but he had no idea how to go about it. Foster care was a poor training ground for marriage or fatherhood.

Then there was his PTSD to deal with. Each time he thought he'd made progress, something would trigger a flash. It made it impossible to think about any kind of relationship. The best he could offer Nicki was to make her life as easy as possible. Starting with the second apartment above the store. The sooner he had it done, the sooner she could move in. He couldn't save her store, but he could save her sanity.

Nicki was in the middle of placing a special order for a customer later that afternoon when she heard someone call out her name. Glancing up from the checkout counter, she smiled when she saw Jacqueline Wheeler and Diane Ashton coming toward her. "Good morning, ladies. What are you doing here? Did you close up shop today?"

The tall, elegant black woman who owned Jacqueline's Boutique on the square waved off the comment. "Cynthia has things under control."

Diane, who owned the Kiddo's Kloset children's store, nodded. "Same here. My assistant can handle things for a while. You should get someone to help, sweetie. None of us can run a business all alone."

A knowing grin appeared on Jacqueline's face. "I hear you have a very nice assistant. The tall, dark and too-handsome-for-his-own-good type."

Diane's eyes widened. "Really? I heard you hired someone but not that he was a hottie."

Nicki started to talk about Ethan, but the man himself chose that moment to walk onto the sales floor, looking every bit the way her friend had described him. He stopped at the counter and smiled at the ladies. Nicki's cheeks turned pink. There was no way she could deny how attractive he was. She introduced Ethan to the ladies, cringing when neither of her friends made an effort to hide their appreciation.

"So what can I do for you?"

Jacqueline blinked and looked at her. "Oh. We brought

you some things for the sidewalk sale." She laid a large poster on the counter. The colorful images and bold lettering proclaimed the excitement of the upcoming Square Fair. "Hang this in the front window so everyone will see it as they pass by."

Diane placed a stack of smaller notices on the counter. "And these are flyers for you to stuff in customers' bags along with their purchases."

"Thank you. I'll make sure we use these." Ethan picked up the poster, removed a roll of tape from the drawer and headed to the window.

"I think this is going to be our best Square Fair ever. I'll have three racks of clothing from my boutique out front, and everything in the store will be marked down twenty percent that day. You'll have to come by and shop."

Nicki would love nothing more. "I'm hoping I'll be too busy myself to leave the store."

Diane touched her arm. "Well, you must slip away and see all the precious baby clothes I'm putting out on the sidewalk. You won't want to miss these deals for that little princess of yours."

"I'll try my best."

Diane leaned in close. "I'll put back several things for you to look at. You can come in on Monday. I'll honor the sale price for you."

"Thank you. That's very sweet."

Jacqueline stretched out her hand. "Oh, I forgot to tell you. Angie Durrant said a reporter from the *Clarion-Ledger* newspaper in Jackson is coming down to do a feature about the Square Fair. And she said one of the local TV stations will be here to cover the events that day."

Diane clasped her hands together. "Praise God. This will raise so much money for our shelters."

Nicki's hope soared. She'd counted on the sidewalk sale to shore up the store's bottom line, but with the added publicity, she was beginning to think it might mean a real turnaround.

She approached Ethan as soon as the women left. "Did you hear what they said? The fair is drawing people from Jackson and probably the surrounding areas like Madison, Brandon and Clinton. This could be the answer to my prayers."

Ethan replaced the tape in the drawer, then rested his elbows on the counter. "I hope so. I know how much you want this store to survive."

She sighed and laid her hand over his. "It has to. My parents are depending on me. I know I can't count on the sidewalk sale to save Latimer's, but it could give us a big boost."

Ethan touched his finger to the tip of her nose, making her smile. "Not unless we get this new floor plan together in time. I'd better get back to work."

Nicki smiled as she watched him go. Without Ethan's help and support, she would be floundering. He kept her focused and moving forward. She was starting to depend on him more and more. But she had to be careful not to depend on him too much. Her goal was to rebuild her confidence and regain her belief in herself. Gathering up the pieces of her brokenness was harder than she'd expected. But she refused to give up. Though there were moments when leaning on Ethan's broad shoulders was very tempting.

Rain postponed painting the shelves for the next two days, but Friday dawned clear and warm, and Ethan managed to get caught up. The delay had cut into his work on Nicki's apartment, so he called in reinforcements. His buddies from the PTSD group arrived the moment Nicki drove off after work.

Tearing down the wall between the living room and kitchen was a bigger job than Ethan wanted to tackle on his own. Fortunately, Joe and Bobby both had construction experience. The job was completed without any complications, but it was past midnight and they still had to clean up.

Ethan pulled the six-pack of soda from his fridge and started back to the apartment across the hall. He tossed one to each man.

Ron caught his with a frown and a pointed stare. "This is it? We get one soda for all this work?" The others chuckled.

Ethan grinned and tossed another can over to Stan. "I fed you pizza and those chocolate-chip cookies from that lady you're always talking about."

"Miss Edith."

Joe tilted his cap back with a frown. "Right. This is supposed to be a service project, remember?"

"Since when is helping out a pretty lady a service?" Bobby tossed a grin over his shoulder.

Stan nodded in agreement. "Yeah, if you ask me, this project is all about Ethan getting that pretty lady to live across the hall from him."

Ethan ducked his head to keep the guys from seeing the blush on his cheeks. He was worried that having her near him all the time would be dangerous. She already scrolled through his mind like an endless slide show.

Bobby nudged Ethan's shoulder as he walked past. "Yeah, I think the only service being done here is helping Ethan score points."

Ron moved to his side, a quizzical look on his face. "Are they right? Do you care for this woman?"

"We're friends. Coworkers. Nothing more."

"Have you told her about your PTSD?"

Ethan placed his cordless screwdriver in his toolbox, avoiding his friend's probing look. "No. She doesn't need to know about that. She wouldn't understand."

"Ethan, whether your relationship develops or not, you need to get that out in the open. You know that."

Loud banging on the outside door halted the discussion.

"Dover police. Open up."

Ethan exchanged puzzled looks with his friends before hurrying out to the back door. A uniformed officer stood in the glow of the landing light, one hand resting lightly on his holstered weapon. "What's the problem, Officer?"

"The problem is no one is supposed to be on the premises. Care to tell me what you're doing here and who else is with you?"

"Yes, of course. Come in. My friends and I are fixing up the apartment for the owner."

The officer—Captain Ty Durrant, according to his name tag—looked skeptical.

"Is that so? Well, when I called her, she didn't know anything about it."

Ethan's heart sank. "You called Nicki?"

"It's my job to notify business owners when there are trespassers on their property."

Footsteps on the wood floors drew the cop's attention. His stern expression eased into a smile as he looked past Ethan. "Ron. What are you doing here?"

"I was going to ask you the same thing. Guys, this

is Captain Durrant. Stan Arnold, Joe Ford, Bobby Edmonds and Ethan Stone. He lives here."

"Oh, you must be the new assistant Nicki took on. Sorry to interrupt your party, but when I drove by and saw all the cars and the lights, I called Nicki and she didn't seem to know anything about it."

Ethan ran a hand through his hair. "It was supposed to be a surprise."

"Sorry. But with all the robberies going on, it's my job to question anything that looks out of place."

"Any leads on that?" Ron asked.

"A few."

"Hey, I hear congratulations are in order."

Ethan watched as a huge smile appeared on the cop's face, and he stood a little taller.

"Yeah. It's great news."

"Boy or girl?"

"Don't know yet. We'll find out next week."

The sound of the back door opening drew the men's attention. Nicki rushed toward them, stopping in her tracks and staring at Ethan. "What's going on? Why are all these men here?"

She glanced at Ty, who smiled and gestured to the men. "Seems they were working on a project and didn't bother to tell anyone. If you're okay with this, I'll be on my way. I'll leave the explanations to you, Stone."

She nodded, but Ethan could see the fear and puzzlement in her eyes. He'd messed up. He could only pray she'd understand. He should have told her what he was doing instead of trying to surprise her.

"Someone tell me what's going on."

His friends drifted back to the apartment, allowing

them privacy. He wasn't sure if he was grateful or irritated. He could use some backup.

"Ethan. Tell me what's going on."

Nicki stared at Ethan, waiting for some explanation. After getting Ty's call, she'd raced over here, horrible scenarios swirling around in her mind. Had the robbers hit the store? Had Ethan tried to stop them and been injured? Why were there so many cars out back? She didn't recognize any of them. She turned to Ethan once more.

Ethan took her arm and led her to the second apartment, where the men were gathering up tools and equipment. The place looked different somehow, but she was too upset to process that now.

"I suppose I'd better introduce you. These are the guys from my prayer group at Hope Chapel."

Ethan rattled off names, but Nicki was too befuddled for any of them to register.

"I asked them here to help me finish up."

"Finish up what?"

He motioned her deeper into the apartment, gesturing with one hand. As she stepped into the living area, she gasped. The outdated apartment had been transformed. The mauve carpet was gone, revealing wooden floors polished to a shine. The hideous borders along the ceiling were gone and a fresh coat of pale green paint made the room warm and soothing.

"It's for you and Sadie."

Finished collecting their tools, the men filed out with nods to her and smiles directed at Ethan. Nicki looked around the space again, unable to find words to express her surprise. She turned to Ethan. "You did this for me?"

"I know how important it is to have a place of your own." He broke eye contact and moved farther into the room. "We're not done painting. I'll finish that tomorrow. Then you can move in whenever you're ready. Sadie's room is done."

Happy anticipation flew through her. Inside the small second bedroom, she pressed her fingertips to her lips, overcome with joy. The room was the perfect shade of pink. She could already see where the crib would go. "It's beautiful. Sadie will love this." She looked at Ethan, who was leaning against the doorjamb watching her, a pleased smile on his face.

"Her mom's room is ready, too."

Brushing past him, she crossed to the master bedroom, smiling at the fresh, inviting feel of the room. Light from the arched windows would flood the room in the daytime. Happiness and surprise bubbled up from inside. "I never would have believed that the apartment could look like this. How long have you been working on it?"

Ethan shrugged. "Not that long, really. Taking out the wall in the kitchen took the longest. I needed help with that."

"Does my father know about this?"

"All done with his approval."

She faced him, her heart so full of appreciation she didn't know whether to laugh or cry. "Why did you do this?"

"You're under a lot of pressure. You deserve a place of your own. This seemed like the best solution."

"Thank you." Tears welled up in her eyes. This kind, thoughtful man had gone out of his way to provide a home for her and Sadie. The depth of his consideration was almost too much to grasp. How could she ever tell him how much his gesture meant to her? Getting out of her parents' home was exactly what she needed. Impulsively, she hugged him. His hands rested lightly on her shoulders, but he didn't hug her back. She looked up into his face, his brown eyes a warm chocolate color. In that instant she realized she wanted to kiss him. He must have read her thoughts because as she inched closer, he took her shoulders in his hands and held her still.

"Don't. Unless you mean it," he whispered.

What did he mean? Did he want the real thing? If so, did that mean he had feelings for her? She held his gaze, rose on tiptoe and kissed his cheek. His dark eyes warmed.

"It's late. You'd better go home."

"This is the nicest thing anyone has ever done for me. I'll never be able to repay you for your kindness."

He trailed a finger along her cheek. "Just be happy. That'll be more than enough."

Chapter Eight

Nicki watched from the upper landing of the back stairs of Latimer's Sunday afternoon as Ethan and Jerry Gordon unloaded the final pieces of furniture from the bed of Jerry's truck. Finally, she had a place of her own. Her own kitchen, her own space. Her own life.

Debi appeared at her shoulder. "Jerry figured four trips to get everything moved from your mom's, but it only took three."

"They're good. Maybe they should start their own moving company."

Debi nodded. "It sure would be safer than being a cop."

Nicki watched Ethan carry the rocking chair with the same ease he did boxes and fixtures in the store. He glanced up and caught her eyes, sending a rush of warm embarrassment into her cheeks. She went inside to make sure the space was clear for the chair. She found herself searching Ethan out, stopping to watch him as he worked. She told herself it was because she was interested in the work he was doing in the store. Truth was, she couldn't ignore him.

Thanks to Debi and Jerry's help, they'd accomplished

the move in an afternoon. But having Ethan moving about her place had created too many opportunities for them to bump into one another. So much so, they'd quit making apologies and turned it into a running joke.

"Do you have everything out of your car?" Debi came toward her from the kitchen.

Nicki nodded, looking away from Ethan as he disappeared down the hall with the rocker.

"Okay, well, we need to go, then. Jerry's mom has the kids and he's on duty tonight."

Nicki gave her friend a hug. "I can't thank you enough for all your help and the use of the truck."

Jerry walked in with two plastic bags. "That's the last of it."

After warm goodbyes, Nicki closed the door and glanced around at the chaos that was her living room. It was the most beautiful sight she'd ever seen. All it needed to be perfect was Sadie. Sounds coming from the small bedroom reminded her that Ethan was still here.

She stopped in the doorway, watching as he assembled Sadie's crib. He double-checked it, making sure everything was secure. The gesture was so sweet and thoughtful it left a strange lump in her chest. It would be so easy to care for him. He was always waiting to help, but never pushing, always giving her space to make her own decisions, but happy to offer a different idea when needed. She could easily imagine him as part of her life, offering a shoulder to lean on and a hand to hold at the end of the day.

He stood, giving the crib one last tug before turning and smiling. "I think Sadie should be safe in her bed."

Nicki smiled. He always thought of others first. She'd

forgotten how nice that was. "She's going to love it. Thank you for helping me move, Ethan."

"Jerry and Debi helped, too. You're blessed to have such good friends."

"I am. But so are you. If it weren't for your prayer group, I wouldn't have this apartment."

Ethan bent down and closed the lid on his toolbox. "Is there anything else that needs to be put together?"

Her life, but he couldn't help with that. "I don't think so."

She followed Ethan to the door. He set the toolbox down and scanned the cluttered living room. "You sure I can't help you with some of this stuff?"

Nicki shook her head. "Thanks, but I'm looking forward to finding a special place for everything."

Happiness welled up in her. There had been a time when she'd resigned herself to living with her parents forever. But now she had her own little oasis of privacy. Tears began to stream down her face.

"Ethan, I can never thank you enough for fixing up this apartment. It means everything to me. To have a place where I can do as I please, where no one will find fault or take control—" She smiled before continuing. "It's all because of you. Thank you for having my back, Ethan." She smiled as an old memory surfaced. "When I was learning to ride a bicycle, my dad would steady it until I got on. Then he would let go and let me try on my own. He was always there ready to catch me, but he never interfered. Knowing he was there was enough. Like you do. I appreciate that so much." She thought she saw a flicker of sadness pass through his eyes. Perhaps it was because he had never experienced the love of a father in his life.

"You deserve a place of your own." He tucked her

hair behind her ear, letting his fingers trail through the strands, sending a shiver down her arms. The look in his eyes drew her closer, but she pulled away. While she was growing to care more and more for Ethan, she wasn't sure she could handle a relationship right now. She had to concentrate on her and Sadie's future, nothing else.

Didn't she?

It was a question that was getting harder and harder to answer.

Ethan stared out his apartment window, his mind replaying Nicki's story about her father from the night before. The message was clear. She appreciated his friendship, but that was all it was. Yet when they were together, he knew she was as drawn to him as he was to her. It was why he'd warned her away the other night. He'd realized he was starting to care and he wasn't interested in a friendly kiss. He wanted her to care about him.

Which meant he needed to take Ron's advice. If he hoped for any kind of relationship with Nicki, he had to tell her about his PTSD. He'd spent all night and most of today weighing the pros and cons of opening up to her. Working together these past few weeks had created a deep bond between them. His heart was losing the battle to stay clear of emotional entanglements with her and Sadie. Telling her his situation could end all of that. She might even ask him to leave.

But not telling her could cause the same result. Nicki had hinted that her ex had been secretive, manipulative. She wouldn't be happy to know he'd hidden something like this from her.

But maybe that was for the best. The attraction between them was growing even if neither of them was willing to acknowledge it. Revealing his PTSD to Nicki would either end their relationship or push it forward. Either way, it was time to see where things were headed.

His gaze drifted to the closet in the living room, where he'd stored a box he'd found when he'd cleaned the apartment. It held personal items that he'd meant to ask Nicki about. Maybe that would be a good way to start his talk.

Retrieving the box, he carried it across the hall and knocked on her door. The smile on her face when she saw him buoyed his spirits. It took him a moment to find his voice. "I have something for you."

She glanced at the box. "What is it?"

"Not sure. But I thought you'd better look."

She stepped back to allow him to enter. "You can put it by the sofa."

He placed the box on the floor between the sofa and the easy chair. Sadie was nowhere to be found, and his disappointment was stronger than he'd anticipated. "Sadie asleep already?"

"I just put her down. You can go peek at her if you'd like."

Quietly, he made his way to the nursery and stepped to the side of the crib. Sadie was sound asleep. Little fists resting on either side of her head, tiny mouth moving as if still eating in her sleep. He ached to touch her, but didn't want to wake her.

Overcome with a yearning to take her picture, Ethan pulled his cell phone from his pocket and swiped open the camera. His heart skipped a beat as he started to aim it at Sadie. What would he see? He'd promised to never take another picture. He looked at the sleeping baby again, his heart swelling with affection. Slowly, he moved the phone until Sadie was framed in the screen. Nothing happened. All he felt was delight in seeing the little girl. He pressed the button with his thumb, capturing the image. Maybe looking through the frame of a phone wasn't the same as looking through the lens of his camera.

Sliding the phone back into his pocket, he quietly eased out of the room and rejoined Nicki.

He sat in the easy chair, glancing at the few items she'd already removed from the box. Comic books, a baseball cap and two trophies.

"This box is filled with my brother's things. Where did you find it?"

The tremor in her voice moved him. "It was behind the computer boxes. I slid it into the closet and forgot about it."

"I wonder why it's here?"

"Maybe your parents brought it over."

She shook her head. "But Kyle might have the last time he was home. I remember he talked about moving into one of these apartments when he got out of the service. He only had one year left, but he never made it home."

Ethan touched her hand. "I'm sorry."

"He was so different that last visit. He was distant and somber. Not at all like his old self."

Ethan steeled himself and faced her. "Being over there changes a man."

"I suppose. He had the strangest look in his eyes. Sometimes he'd just stare into the distance like he was miles away and seeing something else, and—"

She looked at him, her eyes widening. "It's the same look I see in your eyes. It's not just being in the war zone. It's more, isn't it?"

Ethan clasped his hands together between his knees.

Where to begin? "Nicki, I suspect your brother may have been suffering from PTSD. Post-traumatic—"

"I know what it means. Why didn't he tell us?"

"Maybe he didn't know."

She looked at him for some explanation.

"When you realize what's happened, it's usually too late."

Nicki looked into the box, pulling out a well-used baseball glove. "I knew something was wrong, but he wouldn't talk to me. Maybe I could have helped."

"Doubtful. People who suffer from PTSD need professionals who understand the disorder. Did your brother play pro ball? That's a quality glove."

She nodded. "One year in the minors, but then he decided he wanted to join the marines. Did you play?"

"A few years in college."

She stared at the old leather glove a long moment. "You suffer from PTSD too, don't you?"

His throat tightened. "Yes. But I had help, and I've learned to manage the worst of it."

"What happened to you?"

"I was a photographer with TNZ News, embedded with the troops in several war zones. One day there was an explosion." He paused. "I couldn't do it anymore. Too many horrific images… I broke."

She touched his hand, her eyes filled with compassion. "I never thought about how war would affect a journalist. Is that why you left all those blanks on your application? You didn't want me to know?"

"Sometimes people get the wrong idea about PTSD. They think we're all time bombs waiting to go off."

"Is that where the scars came from? The explosion?"

He nodded.

"But you're better now?"

"Yes. I still have the occasional nightmare and a flash of memory now and then. Still haven't picked up my camera again. Not sure what I'll see when I look through the viewfinder."

"And flashbacks?"

Ethan swallowed. He wanted to be truthful, but it was proving harder than he'd anticipated. "Few and far between, and I have a support group."

She frowned. "You do?"

"The guys that helped finish this place, they're not just a prayer group—they're the PTSD support group. We meet once a week."

She looked at him a moment, then stood and walked across the room, clutching the baseball glove to her chest. "You didn't think I'd understand? Or did you think I'd ask you to leave?"

"I didn't know. Like I said, people react differently. I didn't want to scare you."

"I'm glad you told me. It explains a lot of things."

"But does it change anything between us? I'll leave if you're worried. I don't want to add to your burden, Nicki."

She kept her back to him for a long moment, then turned to face him. "I don't know how I feel. It's a lot to take in. I guess I need time to think about it."

He moved toward her, his heart in pain when she stepped back, clutching the glove more tightly. She obviously didn't want to be near him right now.

"I'm going to go. I'll be at work in the morning unless you want to make changes. Good night." Ethan closed the door behind him, praying it wasn't the last time he crossed her threshold.

Nicki watched the door close behind Ethan, her heart pulling in different directions. Ethan had PTSD. What exactly did that mean? Was he like the characters she saw on television? Those ticking time bombs that might turn violent at any moment, like Ethan had mentioned? Her stomach knotted at the thought. But she'd worked with him for weeks now. He wasn't a violent man. She'd witnessed his gentleness every day, in the way he held Sadie and the way he interacted with her. Ethan possessed a quiet, controlled strength, the kind a woman could depend on for protection. Ethan said he'd had professional help dealing with his disorder. That was good, wasn't it?

All his friends suffered, too. And her brother. Moving to the box, she sorted through the remaining items. A team shirt, a yearbook, news clippings, a copy of a Michael Crichton novel. Things a guy might want to keep to remember good times. But Kyle was gone now. She'd ask her parents if they wanted this stuff. She looked at the baseball glove in her hand. Ethan had said he loved the game. She'd give him the glove.

She was afraid to trust her instincts about men, but she knew in her heart Ethan wasn't a threat or a danger. She wanted him here, across the hall, helping her in the store. Despite her good intentions, she'd grown to depend on him. More than that, she'd come to care for him. A lot.

She'd seen the raw hurt in his brown eyes when she'd told him she needed time to think about what he'd told her. She didn't want him worrying about this all night. Picking up the glove, she crossed the hall and knocked on his door. The tension she saw in his posture when he opened the door made her glad she'd come. "Ethan, I want you to have Kyle's glove."

He looked puzzled. "Are you sure?"

"Positive. And I have a lot of work for you to do

in the morning." As she handed the glove to him, she saw the realization dawn on his face, the light returning to his eyes.

"Nicki, I'll understand if you—"

She shook her head. "I'm sure about that, too." Walking back to her apartment, she found herself wondering again what it would be like to kiss him. Ethan had started to invade her thoughts. His quiet confidence and soft-spoken tone reminded her of her father. Ethan was a compelling man, a strong man in character and in body. It would be so easy to let him fight her battles. But that was not in her nature. Which was why she needed to focus on her task and keep all romantic, nonsensical thoughts about her employee in the far corners of her mind.

Ethan knocked on the partially opened door to Nicki's apartment. They had been going back and forth between the two dwellings so often the past few days, they'd taken to leaving the doors open. He'd started helping with the baby, mostly keeping her entertained so Nicki could cook or work. He'd even mastered diaper-changing. Bottle-feeding was best. He liked holding the little girl close.

But he was worried about Nicki. They were behind schedule due to the rain. The sidewalk sale was two days away and they still had a lot to do. Nicki was overworked and trying to hide it behind her smile, but he could see the fatigue. When he didn't get a response to his knock, he tried again and heard Nicki shout from the bedroom. "I'll be right out."

He smiled as he walked into the living room and saw Sadie lying on the floor under the baby gym, the music and bright moving objects capturing her attention. He hunkered down at the edge of the quilt. "Hey, Lady

Sadie. Do you like your new toy?" The baby blinked and looked in his direction and smiled at him. His heart warmed. Reaching out, he touched his finger to her little cheek, then her tiny hand. She grasped it in her fist, kicking her legs and cooing. Did that mean she was happy to see him?

"She adores that thing." Nicki emerged from the hallway. "It keeps her occupied so I can get dressed and have breakfast."

Sadie moved her head at the sound of her mother's voice, arching her back in an attempt to roll over. "Hey, she almost did it."

Nicki knelt down beside Ethan and stroked the baby's head. "It won't be long. I can't wait to see her sit up and crawl and walk. I'm looking forward to every new phase."

Ethan drank in the sight of his lovely landlord. When she looked at Sadie, or talked about her, a beautiful glow came over her face. He looked away. Watching her did strange things to his emotions. Nicki conjured up feelings he wasn't comfortable with. He bent one knee, holding it with his laced fingers. "Next thing you know, you'll be childproofing the apartment."

Nicki glanced around the room, her expression turning serious. "I'll be gone by then."

Ethan swallowed his disappointment. Nicki had made no bones about her leaving town as soon as possible, but each time he heard her say the words aloud, it stung. His foster-care upbringing had left him with a life filled with short-term relationships. He should be used to it, but knowing that Nicki would be leaving had put a barbed thorn in his heart.

"Are you sure that's what you want to do? You have your family here. Friends. People who care about you."

"I know, but I'm perfectly capable of taking care of

myself. I like being independent. Is that so wrong?"
Nicki stood up and walked to the kitchen.

Ethan followed Nicki and took the tea pitcher from
the fridge, pouring himself a glass. There was more
behind Nicki's fierce need for independence than she
was telling him. "No, it's not. I think everyone should
be capable of taking care of themselves. But being totally alone isn't all it's cracked up to be. I grew up that
way, independent, making my own choices. It would
have been nice to have someone to help now and then."

"I appreciate what you're saying, but being on my
own again is important to me."

"Okay, but remember, you're not really alone."

"I know, and I appreciate you being here for me."

Ethan placed his glass in the sink. "I was talking
about your faith."

"Oh, yes. Of course."

Her expression ignited another round of questions
about Nicki's real motivations. He wanted to beg her
to rethink her plan, but her mind was made up, and he
knew he couldn't change it. "It's late and I know you're
tired."

Nicki followed him to the door, smiling at him. She
rested a small hand on his chest, which sent his heart
pounding.

"Thank you for everything. I can't tell you how much
having you here has meant to me. I'm grateful every
day that you walked into my store."

Ethan looked into her eyes and felt himself sinking
into the blue depths. She drew him like no other woman
ever had. His gaze drifted to her slightly parted lips
and he wanted to kiss her. Slowly, he lowered his head.
Then common sense prevailed. Kissing Nicki would be
a huge mistake for both of them. She had a goal and

he wasn't going to be the one to throw her off track. It would also draw him deeper into her life and he was already worried he was in too deep.

With a slight shift of his head, he kissed her cheek. Then he smiled and backed out the door. "Good night."

Ethan swiveled on the stool at the work counter when Nicki walked into the stockroom the next day. Her hair, which usually hung free around her shoulders, had been pulled back with a dark headband, clearly revealing the concern in her eyes. The stress of getting the store ready for the sidewalk sale was evident.

She stopped at his side, peering into the box he'd just opened. "Is that the designer stationery I've been waiting for? I told you to let me know the moment it arrived."

He arched his eyebrows at her harsh tone. "UPS just dropped it off."

She pressed her lips together and shook her head. "Sorry. I'm frazzled today. There's still so much to do and not much time left."

"It'll get done." Leaning to the side, he picked up the pricing gun. Maybe putting her in charge of the merchandise would make her feel more in control. He swung his arm toward her. She flinched, throwing her arms up over her head. "Nicki?"

She lowered her arms, but kept her fists at her neck. Waves of fear emanated from her body, shredding his soul. He reached for her again, but she shrank away. His stomach knotted. What had happened to her? He had a sick feeling he knew, but didn't want to believe it.

"I'm sorry. I didn't mean to scare you." He laid the pricing gun on the workbench.

She stared at him, her blue eyes filling with tears. "I'm sorry."

He shrugged. "Nothing to be sorry about." He saw her start to tremble and pushed the other stool toward her. "Why don't you sit down?"

She nodded and perched on the stool, staring at her hands a long moment. "I'm sorry. I thought…" She took a breath. "Never mind what I thought."

Ethan reached out and stroked her arm. "You thought I was going to hit you."

She nodded, head bowed. It was all he could do to maintain control of his anger. He willed himself to remain calm for Nicki's sake.

"Did your husband hit you?"

She didn't respond, only continued to stare at her hands.

"It helps to talk about it." He waited, knowing it was best to let her tell the story in her own time.

Finally she looked up, her eyes moist. "How could I be so stupid? I thought I was an intelligent woman, but I let him take over until I had nothing left. I just didn't see it until he—" She drew a shaky breath. "Brad wanted me with him all the time. I even quit my job. His attention seemed so sweet and romantic at first, but then he began to cut me off from my friends and family until I was completely isolated and under his control. I couldn't make a decision or a choice without his okay."

A sob escaped her throat, increasing the tears. "I didn't even know my father was sick."

Ethan stood and pulled her close, resting his chin on the top of her head.

"The verbal abuse had been going on for a while, but when I got pregnant he changed and became more and more angry. When I was four months pregnant with Sadie, I told him I wanted to go home to see my parents, and he became furious. It was the first time he'd ever— I couldn't let him hurt the baby. I called my attorney and she made all the arrangements for my escape. I left that night. All I could take was a small bag of clothes. I didn't even take my cell phone so he couldn't track me down."

"Did he come after you?"

"No. I found out later that my husband was under investigation by the FBI. I guess he decided to cut his losses and flee the country. A week after I left him, I learned he'd been killed in a plane crash trying to flee to the Caribbean."

Ethan squeezed her hand. "I'm glad you and Sadie got away." It all made sense now. Nicki's fierce determination to be on her own, the odd comments she'd made about her husband. She must have felt as if she'd left one confining life for another. Being trapped in her marriage, then coming home only to be trapped into saving her family's store.

"I should have left sooner. I suspected he was seeing other women, but he kept telling me how much he loved me. And I wanted to believe it because I had given up everything for him. It was only later that I realized I hadn't given up anything. He'd taken it all from me. And I'd let him."

She met his eyes. "I'm sorry I reacted that way. I know you wouldn't hit me, but for a moment I was back there."

"Flashback," he said, and her eyes widened with realization. "You don't have to have been through a war to experience one."

Nicki reached out and pulled a paper towel from the worktable. "I always thought of myself as strong, capable, smart. Now I'm not sure who I am anymore."

He nodded. "The things that happened in the Middle East made me question who I was. I thought I was immune to the horrors of war. I liked being a photographer because I could see others' emotions, but I didn't have to experience them myself. I found out differently. I came to Dover to figure out who I'm going to be from now on."

"Guess we're not too different. We're both having to redefine who we are."

"Do your parents know about this?" Sometime during their conversation Nicki had grasped both of his hands, holding them tightly. He liked being connected to her.

"No. I never told them the real story."

"Why?"

"They'd be so disappointed in me. My mom adored Brad. She thought I'd married so well. I couldn't tell her. It was the only thing I ever did that she approved of. And my dad would be heartbroken. He always said I was so intelligent and perceptive. He'd never understand how I could have allowed myself to be dominated that way."

"Your folks strike me as understanding people. They might be surprised, but I don't think they'll be ashamed of you."

Nicki released his hands and stepped away. "I'll tell them eventually, but right now I have to focus on saving the store."

"To prove to yourself you are capable or to prove to them you're worthy of their love?"

Nicki frowned and swiped tears from her cheeks. "No, that's not it at all. But after being a prisoner for so long, I want to prove to myself that I can stand on my own and take care of myself."

She sighed, running her hands through her hair. "What's wrong with me? How could I have been so blind?"

"There's nothing wrong with you. You're a loving, trusting woman."

"Naive and gullible, more like."

"No." He pulled her into his embrace again. "Those are qualities to admire, not be ashamed of." He inhaled the floral scent of her hair into his lungs. He wanted to stay here forever, holding her, being her champion. But he wasn't the man she needed any more than her husband had been. Nicki wanted a man like her father, a family man, a man who could be a father to little Sadie, and that wasn't him.

The doorbell sounded, and Nicki swiped at her wet cheeks again. "Customers."

"I'll get it. You stay here." Ethan hurried out front, marveling again at Nicki's strength and courage. He had no doubt that she'd make her dream come true and raise Sadie to be an accomplished young lady. But a small part of him wished she were a little less strong. Then she might need him in her life.

After Ethan left, Nicki returned to her office and slipped quietly into the back room, where Sadie was sleeping. Sinking to the floor, she gazed at her little girl, drawing comfort from the sight. She couldn't believe she'd told Ethan about her abusive husband. She hadn't planned on telling anyone. Ever. But his quiet strength, his understanding attitude, had given her a safe place to finally release the turmoil she'd suppressed all these months.

Drained and shaky, she was still aware of a profound sense of relief and renewed courage. Ethan was right. Talking about her pain did help. But he'd raised another question. Was she trying to prove her worth to her parents by saving Latimer's? Was she overcompensating for her failure by trying to prove she was capable and strong and not the weak woman Brad had dominated?

"You going to be okay?"

She glanced up at Ethan, who stood in the office doorway. The concern in his chocolate eyes chased away her doubts. "As long as I have Sadie, I'm more than okay." She got to her feet and faced him. "Ethan, I'm sorry for falling apart. I'm just overly tired, that's all."

"I know. We've been working pretty hard."

"I appreciate you listening. I didn't realize how much I needed to talk to someone."

"I'm here whenever you need me."

His tender gaze reached into her heart like a warm hug, and she laid her hand on his forearm, needing the connection. She had a feeling she was starting to need him, too. His hands moved up her arms, gently pulling her closer. Her heart skipped a beat, anticipating what was to come.

The front bell shattered the moment. Ethan stepped back, exhaling a heavy sigh. "Want me to get that?"

She shook her head, willing her heart to return to normal. "I'll go. The rain has stopped. You'd better get those last two shelves painted." She watched him leave, a storm of conflicting emotions pulling at her insides. She'd thought he was going to kiss her. She'd wanted him to. She shouldn't, but her attraction to Ethan was undeniable. He was even starting to invade her dreams at night.

He was the kind of man she could love. He always made her feel safe, important and confident. But she wanted to feel those things through her own endeavors and accomplishments. Not simply as the object of someone's affection. That was why she had to save the store. To prove to herself she was strong and capable again.

First, she'd get Latimer's back on track, and then

she'd have time to think about a relationship. But when the time came, she would have moved on and where would Ethan be?

Nicki stepped out onto the sidewalk, inhaling the fresh air and allowing herself a moment to appreciate the baskets, filled with pink and purple petunias, the city had hung from the street lamps. The day was so inviting she'd decided to walk to the bank while Sadie napped, confident Ethan could handle anything that came up. Nicki walked through the park, taking time to enjoy the beauty in the square. The azaleas were glorious this time of year, and she was glad she was home to experience spring.

Living above the store was proving to be a bigger blessing than she'd anticipated. She was close to all the shops and stores and had access to the park. Having her own place had restored her sense of control and freedom. Having Ethan across the hall had proved beneficial, too. He was always available for brainstorming and advice and had become a good diaper changer. Lately they'd started sharing meals in the evening.

As she neared the First Dover Bank and Trust on the far corner of the square, she noticed preparations for the Square Fair were already under way. Bright red tape laid out in squares marked the locations of the various cook-off contestants. The stores she passed proudly displayed the colorful Square Fair posters. City workers had delivered metal barriers that would be used to block traffic from the main streets. So many people depended on this one day to boost their bottom lines. And she was depending on it to save everything her family had.

Jacqueline Wheeler emerged from her boutique and

waved as Nicki passed by. "Taking a break from the store?"

Nicki smiled as she received a hug from her. "It's too pretty a day to waste inside."

"It's going to be even better tomorrow. I wanted to let you know that Diane's store was nearly robbed last night. The police saw them, but the rascals got away again. Chief Reynolds said they're getting close to catching them. I just wish they'd hurry up."

Though worried about the unsolved robberies, Nicki refused to be discouraged as she completed her banking then made her way back to the store and into her office. She was too excited about the sidewalk sale and the possibilities it offered.

Cooing sounds from the baby monitor told Nicki nap time was over. She retrieved her little girl, cradling her close as she walked back to the front. Sadie was starting to develop a personality. She was happy and curious and liked to mimic the sounds she heard.

Glancing up as the bell over the front door jingled, Nicki was surprised to see her father walk in. Her concern quickly dissipated when she saw him smile and noticed the healthy color of his skin. He was recuperating quickly from the transplant.

"Daddy, what are you doing here? Where's Mom?" Her father made a beeline for Sadie, taking her from Nicki and cuddling her close.

"I'm supposed to walk each day, and I got tired of looking at the same houses in the neighborhood, so I decided I'd walk the square. Your mother's getting her hair done."

Nicki slipped her arm under her dad's and rested her head briefly on his shoulder. "I'm so glad. The store doesn't feel right when you're not here." Her father looked away from his granddaughter for a moment and scanned the store.

"Well, I'll be a bluetick hound. This place certainly has changed."

She tensed. "Are you upset?"

He smiled down at her. "No. I think you're doing an amazing job. It's just a surprise. I never realized how dull my store had become." He hugged her shoulder with his free arm. "You're doing a wonderful job. This will bring in customers just wanting to see all the changes."

Nicki warmed with the compliment. "Things are getting better, Dad. Not as fast as I'd like, but given a little more time I think we can put Latimer's back in the black."

Her father pinned her with a curious look. "'We'? You mean you and Ethan?"

"Yes. If it wasn't for my Ethan I couldn't have done any of this. He's been such a blessing."

"*Your* Ethan?"

Nicki blushed and shook her head. "I meant in an employee kind of way. Nothing else."

"I see."

Nicki swallowed the tightness in her throat. "After all, he's the one who figured out how to reconfigure the old shelving for my new floor plan, and he's given me a lot of good ideas on how to generate business."

"He's a good man. I like him." He handed the baby back to Nicki. "Think I'll say hello. Then I'd better get going. Your mom won't be happy if I'm late." He kissed her forehead and walked toward the stockroom.

Nicki watched him, trying to decide if he really wanted to talk to Ethan or if he was merely stalling and not ready to go home. He'd had that penetrating stare that always told her he knew something she didn't. She hoped it wasn't some crazy notion that she and Ethan were an item. They were friends. Nothing more. So why couldn't she forget his tender support yesterday when she'd confessed her deepest shame?

She didn't know what to do. Being cared for by Ethan felt nothing like the so-called "love" she'd received from Brad. Ethan gave freely from a generous and caring heart. But she wasn't looking for a connection at this point in her life. Though she was beginning to wonder if her heart had other ideas...

Chapter Nine

Ethan unpacked the electronics display that had arrived yesterday. It was larger than he'd expected, but not complicated to assemble. Latimer's didn't have the space or budget to stock a large supply of electronic equipment, so the company had provided a sample kiosk where customers could examine several devices, order them and have them shipped to their homes later.

He'd have to check with Nicki to see if she'd decided where to place it in the store. It was attractive and should draw customers to examine the sample laptop, eReader, smartphone and small digital camera. Ethan let his gaze rest on the box that held the small silver camera. For the first time in nearly a year, he had a desire to take a few shots. He wished he'd taken some before and after pictures of Latimer's. It had changed a lot since he'd started working there.

The push to get everything done in time for the sidewalk sale was taking a toll. Several items Nicki had counted on for the big event hadn't arrived yet. He was working hard to get it all done, but Nicki was pushing herself even more, and he was worried about her.

"Looks like my girl is keeping you on your toes."

Ethan smiled when he saw Allen Latimer coming into the stockroom. He looked much stronger than he had the last time they'd met.

"Afternoon, sir. What brings you here?"

"Change of scenery. And some time with the two prettiest ladies in town."

Ethan smiled and shook the man's hand. "You'll get no argument from me. Sadie is a beauty."

Latimer strode to the workbench. "Just like her mother."

"Yes, sir." He had the strangest feeling Mr. Latimer was on a fishing expedition. "You're a blessed man."

"Don't I know it. I was telling my daughter how great the store looks. I wanted you to know how much I appreciate all you've done for my girl. She can be bullheaded like her mother, and she doesn't like to ask for help."

"I've noticed." He grinned in agreement.

"But she'll take help from you. Why do you suppose that is?"

Ethan's neck suddenly felt tight. "I couldn't say. Things were pretty serious when I showed up. I suppose she was desperate."

Mr. Latimer nodded thoughtfully. "True." He glanced around the stockroom. "Don't think I've ever seen the place so neat. I could never find anything in here, but then, Charlie had his own system. I used to be better about staying on top of things, but after I lost my boy, and I got sick..." He shrugged. "Guess I let things go."

"I understand, sir. Illness steals your energy. All you can do is try to survive. Everything else fades into the background."

"You speaking from experience?"

Ethan hesitated. Apparently Nicki hadn't told her father about his PTSD. "Yes, sir."

Latimer studied him a moment. "You strike me as

an observant man. Someone who watches, and thinks things through before acting."

"I suppose so. I like to take my time. Look at things before I jump in."

"My daughter is very fond of you."

"I don't know if I'd say that. We're friends. Coworkers."

"So you don't find her attractive?"

Ethan frowned, suddenly feeling like a prom date being grilled by the father before taking his daughter to the dance. He struggled to find a proper response. If he said yes, Latimer might read more into it. There was nothing between him and Nicki. The attraction was there. He wouldn't deny that, but her plans for the future didn't include staying in Dover. If he said no, he'd be insulting the man's child. He attempted a middle ground. "She's very attractive. Any man would think so."

"She has feelings for you. More than just as a friend."

"Oh, no, sir. I think you're wrong about that."

Latimer chuckled softly. "Then you're not as observant as I thought you were." He waved and walked out, leaving Ethan to puzzle over the comment. Did Nicki care for him in a romantic way? And if so, what did he do about it? More important, how did he feel about it? Nicki was the most fascinating woman he'd ever met, but he wasn't ready for a permanent relationship. He had to get his life on track before he could think about his future.

But more and more, when he thought about his future, it seemed to include Nicki and Sadie.

Nicki stood in the middle of Latimer's the morning of the sidewalk sale, looking around slowly so she could take in all the changes. The store looked amazing. Fresh and different.

"What do you think, Sadie? Will the people of Dover like our do-over?" she whispered to her daughter, who was snuggled in her arms. Back in her office, she settled Sadie in her carrier beneath the play gym she'd purchased especially for today, hoping it would keep her entertained while she waited on the hundreds of customers she anticipated today.

Please, God, let my hopes be realized. She wanted to make her parents proud. After a quick check of the baby monitor, Nicki went out front. The store would open in less than fifteen minutes. She smiled when she saw Ethan already at work.

"You ready for today?"

"I hope so." She glanced around, mentally checking the items selected to be out front on the sidewalk tables. She and Ethan had prepared the bins and stacked them near the entrance last night so they'd be ready to carry them outside as soon as the sidewalk sale began. But doubts sprang a leak in her confidence. "Maybe this is too much merchandise to offer at once?"

"Then we'll put it out a little at a time."

"Right. But what if it's too little? I don't know if I have anything else to unload."

"If that's the case, then people will want to come back tomorrow to see what else we have. Either way, it's a win-win situation." He smiled. "Don't worry. It'll be fine. You've done a great job. I have confidence in you."

"Thanks." He always made her feel good.

"You'd better get ready. The store opens in ten minutes. I'm going to start moving the tables out front. The furniture store has already started carrying things outside."

"Vicki should be here any minute to help." She was glad she'd listened to Ethan and asked her former part-time employee, college student Vicki Borman, to come in for the sale. She knew the register and the merchandise.

Nicki lost track of time once the store unlocked its doors. A steady stream of shoppers stopped in front of the store to peruse the sale merchandise. By noon, Ethan had replenished the bins twice, and Nicki's hopes were soaring. Thankfully Sadie had been cooperative and taken a long nap.

Nicki finished ringing up a customer's purchase, placed it in a bag, smiled and thanked him sincerely for his business, all the while aware of Sadie's cries on the monitor. She had to break away, but the store was filled with people chatting about the changes to Latimer's and the bargains available on the sidewalks of Dover. It was a huge blessing and she was grateful, but her baby needed her. Scanning the store for Ethan, she waved him over to the register. As he drew near, he glanced at the monitor and understood her unspoken request.

"Go. I've got this."

Nicki thanked him and hurried to the office. In the nursery, Nicki lifted her daughter into her arms, holding her close and speaking softly. A swell of guilt lapped at her mind. If things were different, she could stay with Sadie all the time. But they weren't.

She hated to leave Ethan alone out front, but she had no choice. Soon she'd have to face the fact that Sadie would need more attention than working at the store allowed. Sadie was getting bigger every day and staying awake longer. She'd need toys to stimulate her interest. Toys that made noise and moved, which meant it would be harder to entertain her and still wait on customers, which meant looking into day care. But not yet.

Nicki fixed her a bottle and settled into the chair at her desk, holding Sadie and bottle with one hand. She snagged a piece of fruit with her other hand and scarfed it down. Her new store design was being well received by the shoppers. More than once she'd heard compliments tossed about.

Once the bottle was empty, Nicki stole a moment to cuddle with her little girl. "Are you as excited as I am, sweetheart?"

"Excited about what, Nichelle?"

Nicki spun around, surprised to see her mother coming into the office. "Mom. What are you doing here?"

"I came to see how the sidewalk sale was going, and I found the store packed with customers and no one to assist them."

Nicki swallowed her irritation. "That's not true. Ethan is out there, and Vicki is handling the sidewalk tables." Her mother reached for the baby, and Nicki reluctantly relinquished Sadie.

"Get her things together. I'm taking her home with me for the afternoon."

"Oh, no, Mom. You have enough to do with Dad."

"Nonsense. Your father is doing so well I'm having trouble keeping him from coming back to work."

Nicki hesitated. "I don't know, Mom. Wouldn't she be better here with me?"

Her mother narrowed her eyes and glared. "Nichelle, I've raised two children. I think I can manage to take care of one baby for a couple of hours."

Nicki felt herself giving in. With Sadie out of the store, she and Ethan could concentrate on making this day a success. Nicki quickly shifted mental gears. "Would you like to take the portable crib with you?"

"No. We'll make do."

Nicki scooped up the diaper bag, making sure there were clean bottles and diapers. "She'll play for a while. And she hates to be wet, so be sure and change her often. She'll be ready for a nap around three, and she should sleep for several hours. Call me if you have any trouble." She took a deep breath. "Are you sure you want to do this?"

Her mother's eyes softened. "Sadie is my first grandchild. I haven't had her to myself for more than a moment since she was born. Besides, if you're going to save this store you need to focus on those customers out there and not be distracted by a crying child."

Nicki blinked in surprise. "How did you know?"

"I'm not as blind as you and your father seem to think. But I've learned over the years that it's best if I let him handle things his own way. Your father likes to think he's protecting me. But I always know what's going on."

She'd never heard her mom speak so candidly before. "I thought I was helping you by not letting you babysit Sadie. I didn't want to add to your burden."

Her mother reached out and touched her cheek. "I know. But we miss you and Sadie. This little girl brings a lot of joy to your father and I. Now, give me your car keys because I don't have a carrier in my car. I'll bring her back around closing."

Nicki walked her mother to the car and helped her settle Sadie safely in the baby seat, then stood back as her mother got behind the wheel. Before shutting the door, her mother glanced up at her and smiled. "You've done a good job with the store, Nichelle. It's not what I would have done, but the customers seem to like it."

Speechless, she could only stare as the car disappeared down the alley. If she weren't so busy today, she'd go upstairs and have a good cry. It was the first time she could remember her mother ever paying her a compliment. Back inside, she closed the door and saw Ethan hurrying toward her.

"You okay? You've been gone awhile. Where's Sadie?"

"My mom came and took her home with her." She swallowed the lump in her throat. "Ethan, I think I've made a big mistake."

"What do you mean?"

The doorbell sounded and she gestured toward the front. "Never mind. We have customers to help." There'd be time later to think about what her mother had said.

Ethan locked the front door to Latimer's Office Supply, flipped the sign to Closed and sighed deeply. The sidewalk sale had been a hectic, nonstop event. One he prayed would set the store back on track.

He glanced over at Nicki, who had finished counting the till and was filling out the deposit slip for the bank. He was anxious to learn how the sales added up, but the crease in her forehead and the thin line of her lips told him to hold off for now. He smiled. Nicki Latimer never did anything halfway. It was all or nothing with her. He suspected that when she gave her heart, it would be a forever kind of love.

Shaking off those thoughts, he began sorting out the items stacked inside the door. The store was a disaster. But the good kind.

"Ethan."

When he walked to the counter, there was an odd light in her eyes. "Everything okay?"

She nodded. "More than okay."

He took the deposit slip she handed him and looked at the total sales for the day, stunned at the amount written there. "In one day?"

"Yes." Nicki hurried from behind the counter and threw her arms around his neck.

He held her close, fighting to keep his emotions in check. She fit perfectly against him. She suddenly released him and stepped back.

"Sorry. Got carried away."

Her blue eyes were wide as she searched his face. The pulse in her throat beat like the wings of a hummingbird. She tucked a strand of hair behind her ear.

"Ethan, I think things might be turning around. If we can keep up this kind of traffic in the store, Dad won't have to worry ever again."

Ethan hated to burst her bubble. "But remember, this is only one special day. You probably won't do this much business every day."

Nicki took the slip from his hand and placed it inside the bank deposit bag. "I know. But you heard the shoppers today. They loved the new look of the store, and they were wild about the electronic kiosk."

"I know. I finally had to suggest people come back during the week to browse. There were so many people crowded around it, I couldn't demonstrate it or place orders."

"The main thing is that people see us differently now. They'll start to come here first before going to that big-box store."

Ethan smiled. He loved to see her so confident. "It was all your idea."

"But you helped."

"Naw. All I did was follow orders, boss."

Nicki's blue eyes softened as she held his gaze, sending tiny tingles along his skin. "No, you're more than my employee. You're my friend, and I—"

The back-door buzzer sounded, signaling someone had come inside.

"I'll bet that's my mom."

"I'll start cleaning up."

"No. We can do this tomorrow."

"Tomorrow's Sunday."

"Monday morning, then. I'm too happy to work. I want to celebrate."

Ethan followed Nicki to the back, nodding to Mrs. Latimer before ducking into the stockroom. Nicki wanted to celebrate. So did he. He felt as if he'd been inside this store for weeks. She must feel the same. Maybe he should suggest they take in the events on the square. He'd like to spend time with her outside of the store.

As soon as Mrs. Latimer left, he sought out Nicki in the office. "Do you still want to celebrate?"

"I do. I'm so wound up I'm liable to burst."

"We could walk to the square and try some of that prizewinning catfish. Maybe take in the concert?"

"I would love that. Sadie would, too. She hasn't been in her stroller for days."

After locking the store and retrieving the stroller from upstairs, Ethan assumed pushing duties as they walked to the square.

Nicki inhaled a deep breath. "I love this time of year. All the flowers are blooming, the air is clean and sweet, and the humidity hasn't taken over yet."

Ethan strolled beside her, delighting in her cheerful spirit. He'd never seen her this relaxed and carefree. Nicki absolutely glowed when she was happy. He let the sight of her make a deep impression in his memory. He would always think of her like this.

"So where do you want to eat? Or should I ask whose catfish do you want to try?"

She smiled up at him, bumping his shoulder playfully. "The winner's, of course. I heard Burt Kershaw won this year. He's set up at the other end of the square."

Their journey through the courthouse park was periodically interrupted by old friends, all eager to comment on the new look of the store, inquire about her father and gush over the baby. By the time they arrived at the blue-and-white-striped awning over Kershaw's booth, Ethan's stomach was growling. He pulled out his wallet and handed the man a bill. Nicki reached over and tapped the empty cellophane photograph sleeves.

"Why no pictures?"

He shrugged and took the change the man handed him, quickly closing his wallet and shoving it into his back pocket. "No family." He carried the Styrofoam containers of fried catfish, hush puppies and coleslaw to a picnic table near a giant magnolia. Ethan parked the stroller beside him so Nicki could eat in peace.

She took one bite of the crispy fish fillet and sighed with pleasure. "Oh, Burt definitely deserved the prize. This is so good."

Ethan bit into his fish, nodding in agreement. The fillet was light, the batter tangy and crisp. But as far as he was concerned, spending time with Nicki was the real prize.

Dusk was settling in by the time they finished eating, and the sounds of the band warming up at the other end of the park drifted on the air. Ethan tossed their trash into the bin, then grasped the stroller handle. "Do you want to listen to the concert for a while or are you ready to go home?"

Nicki shook her head, sending her blond waves floating around her neck. "I'm having too much fun. It feels so good to not worry about the store for a change. Besides, my little princess has fallen asleep. We might as well take advantage of this golden opportunity."

The band was beginning their first number, a country tune that invited anyone within earshot to tap their feet in time with the rhythm. As they passed the stately gazebo, a historic structure that had a deep place in the heart of the town, Nicki stopped.

"The music is really loud. Maybe we should sit here in the gazebo and listen for a while."

"All right." Ethan picked up the stroller and carried it up into the gazebo, careful not to wake the baby. Nicki and Ethan sat on the wooden bench that ringed the inside of the bandstand.

Nicki checked on Sadie, then settled back to listen to the band. By the time the third song was under way, darkness was falling and the lights around the roof of the gazebo had blinked on, casting a warm, cozy glow inside. Ethan looked at Nicki. She was even more beautiful in the soft light. All signs of stress had vanished, replaced by a warm glow of happiness. He wished he had his camera with him to capture the moment forever.

Now that they were alone together, Ethan could almost believe there was no one else in town but the three of them. For a brief second, he allowed himself to pretend that Nicki and Sadie were his. That somehow he could be a husband and father, a man who could provide all the love a family needed. Nicki smiled at him and his heart flipped over. He could easily fall in love with this amazing woman. Maybe he already had.

Spring evenings were still cool in late April, and as they walked the few blocks back to the apartment, Sadie needed her blanket. After stowing the stroller in the hallway, Nicki unlocked her apartment and glanced over her shoulder at Ethan. "I'm going to put her down. I'll be right back."

When she returned to her living room, the smile on her face caused a small skip in his pulse. He needed to leave before he did something he might regret.

"How about a cup of coffee?"

He almost said yes, but caught himself in time. "It's been a long day. I'd better go." The look of disappointment on her face both stung and buoyed his spirits. He didn't like to let her down, but he was glad she wanted to spend more time with him.

"But I'm not ready for the day to end."

He smiled. "I have a feeling you'll crash pretty soon."

She sighed and brushed her bangs off her forehead. "I suppose you're right."

He walked to her door, keenly aware of her following close behind him. The gardenia scent she favored wrapped around him, muddling his resolve. When he faced her again, she was only inches away. Her blue eyes were warm and tender, and he found himself unable to look away.

"Thank you for suggesting we take in the fair. I should have been exhausted after today, but I'm too hopeful." She held up her hand. "I know. There's still a long way to go, but it's a great start." She rested her hand on his forearm. "I had fun tonight. It's been a long time since I've been able to forget my problems and just enjoy myself."

"My pleasure." He saw expectation bloom in her eyes and sensed the rising awareness between them. He knew it was time to leave. "Good night." He left before he could rethink this decision.

The street below her apartment window sparkled in the afternoon sun. A few cars passed along the asphalt. A gentle breeze sent the street-lamp flower baskets swaying. A typical Sunday afternoon in Dover. Nicki turned from the window and glanced at her empty apartment. She loved her little home. It had become her refuge at the end of each day, a cozy place to unwind with Sadie.

And Ethan.

But without them, the rooms felt sad and lonely. She'd attended church with her parents this morning, then gone home with them for Sunday dinner. Her mom had offered to watch Sadie so Nicki could clean up the store from the sale. Nicki had jumped at the idea of stealing time alone in her apartment to read or maybe watch a movie. Instead, she'd wandered around like a lost puppy, not knowing what to do with herself.

Her gaze drifted toward the door. Ethan wasn't home. He was involved with some service project. Crossing her hands over her arms, she rubbed them, trying to chase away the lingering chill from last night. She'd thought he was going to kiss her. When she'd thanked him again and rested her hand on his arm, the contact had ignited sparks between them. She'd seen it in his warm chocolate eyes. He was going to kiss her. And she wanted him to. Instead he'd left with only a goodbye, leaving her confused and unsettled and filled with curious feelings.

She knew she was attracted to him and she knew he felt the same, but neither of them was willing to acknowledge it or take the next step. Maybe that was for the best. They were both discovering new directions for their lives. She certainly wasn't looking for a relationship. So why was she always so conflicted when she was with him? Sighing loudly, she grabbed her purse and headed for the door. There was no way she could relax here. Too many questions and too few answers.

Her mom looked up from the sink as Nicki walked

into her parents' kitchen. "You're back early. Everything okay?"

Nicki bent over the baby swing holding Sadie, touching her lovingly. "I missed my little princess."

"Understandable. She's a joy."

"I can't wait until she gets bigger. There's so many things I want to experience with her. Reading stories, tea parties, playing dolls."

Her mother joined her at the table. "I know. I looked forward to all that with you, too. But maybe she'll be like you and not want those things."

Nicki stilled. The sadness in her mother's eyes sent a sharp pain to Nicki's heart. Her mother must have had dreams for her when she was a baby. But Nicki had only wanted to follow her dad around. Tears welled in her eyes. Why hadn't she seen that her mother just wanted to spend time with her? "Mom. I'm so sorry. I must have been a huge disappointment to you."

Her mother frowned. "You were *not* a disappointment. Where did you get such an idea?"

"As long as I can remember, you never liked anything I did. You always wanted me to be more like Kyle."

"Nichelle. I never said that."

"Implied, then."

Her mother took her hand. "I'll admit it was hard sometimes to have a child who was so independent and determined. So many times I wanted to do things with you, but you had your own way, and that was the end of it. Yes, I would have liked more mother-daughter time, but that doesn't mean I didn't love you or approve of you." She smiled. "I just didn't know what to do with you sometimes."

Nicki swallowed the lump in her throat. "I couldn't be like Kyle. He was perfect."

"Hardly. But he was an easier child to raise. He rolled with the punches. If I told him to do something, he did it. When I told you to do something, there was always an argument, a battle."

"Sorry."

"You were always your father's child. Kyle was mine. We understood each other the way you and your dad do."

"Did that hurt you?"

"Sometimes. But why would I be upset because my child adored her father?" Her mother sighed and glanced away. "It's been a rough couple of years. Losing your brother, then Dad getting sick and then you living so far away. I felt like I'd lost both my children. Kyle to death and you to distance. But I took comfort in the fact that you were with a man who could provide the very best for you."

Guilt washed over Nicki's heart. It was time to come clean with her family about the past. "Mom, I think it's time I told you the truth about why I came home."

Chapter Ten

Nicki breezed into the living room Tuesday evening, fastening an earring as she walked. "She's already had her bath, and she's ready for a little playtime. Her formula and bottle are on the kitchen counter. Just shake it up."

Ethan chuckled, holding Sadie a little closer. "I don't think your mommy believes I can take care of you." Nicki frowned. She looked stunning in a slim skirt and soft print top with sleeves that he could describe only as butterfly wings. The pale blues and greens in the pattern set off her blue eyes.

"Of course I do, but I don't know how long this Chamber of Commerce meeting will last. I wouldn't go at all, but I'm anxious to hear how the other stores did after the Square Fair."

"Nicki, I've done this before. Go. You'll be late for the meeting. We'll be fine."

Nicki kissed Sadie goodbye, smiled at him, then hurried out the door.

"Well, Lady Sadie. What should we do first? Want to practice rolling over?" Sadie looked at him and smiled, adding a cute little cooing sound for emphasis. Her eyes sparkled and her hands waved, one finding its way into her mouth. Ethan chuckled. "I promise, we'll celebrate the moment you do." He started to put her down beneath her infant gym, but another idea took hold, one he'd been resisting for a while now.

He wanted pictures of Sadie. He wanted to capture the moment she rolled over for the first time and all her cute little expressions. He'd looked at his cell-phone photo of her a dozen times a day. He'd even added a few more. One shot of Nicki holding Sadie had become his favorite. Nicki's expression of love for her daughter was the most beautiful sight he'd ever seen. But that picture had only made him long for more captured moments.

His cell-phone camera took good pictures, but to get quality shots, he'd have to pick up his professional equipment again. The thought still caused a tightness in his chest. What would he see when he looked through the viewfinder?

Ethan paced the room, bouncing Sadie as he moved. Which did he want more? Pictures of the baby or protecting his emotional well-being? He hadn't had a nightmare in weeks. How did he know it was even at risk if he didn't try? But did he want it bad enough to try looking through the lens?

Sadie cooed and gurgled. He smiled. Maybe she was trying to tell him something. He wanted pictures. He wanted something to have after Nicki left Dover.

In his apartment, he went to the closet in the living room, tugging out the big black case with one hand while juggling Sadie in the other. Hoisting it up on the bed, he opened it and stared at the contents. Three cameras with extra bodies, batteries, converters, chargers, cables, memory cards, cleaning kits and adapters. He waited for the fear to come. It didn't. Encouraged, he pulled out the Canon, his favorite and the most versatile. "Let's see how this works, Lady Sadie."

Back in Nicki's apartment, he laid Sadie beneath the gym, then turned his attention to his camera. His mind automatically analyzed the settings he would need for the amount of light in the room, and he made the adjustments without thinking, each step as familiar as breathing.

Sitting back on his haunches, he placed the camera in his left hand, the weight in his palm like the handshake of an old friend. His right hand folded around the side, his index finger automatically finding the shutter button. His hand trembled. He lowered the camera and turned away. No. It was too risky. *The Lord is my shepherd.*

Taking a deep breath, he raised the camera again and looked through the viewfinder. A rush of air escaped his lungs when all he saw was a baby on a blanket. He pressed the button, capturing Sadie forever. A rush of exhilaration and freedom flooded through him. The world through his lens was under his control. He decided what to shoot, what to zoom in on and what to ignore. This time he was keenly aware of the subject of his photographs. There was a connection that hadn't been there before. A new layer of awareness of what was going on in front of the camera. He noticed when Sadie became tired and rubbed her eyes with tiny fists. Her first whimper pulled the camera away from in front of his face. He set it aside and bent down to pick up the little girl.

Ethan quickly grabbed her bottle and carried her to the rocker. Being a baby model must have worn her out because she took only half her bottle before falling asleep. Cradling her close, he stepped across the hall and placed his camera on the table before carrying Sadie to the nursery. Settling her into her crib, he gently stroked her little head. Did she feel warm? Probably just the heat from the lamps in the living room. He'd switched them all on to get proper lighting.

He spent the next hour looking at the pictures he'd taken, deciding which ones to give Nicki. One thing he'd discovered tonight: the desire to take pictures still lived within him. Not long after Sadie fell asleep, Nicki came home.

"How did the meeting go?" he asked.

"Great. Everyone had huge sales Saturday. We raised a nice sum for the charities." She walked past him, into the bedroom, returning with a small smile. "I guess everything went okay while I was gone?"

"Yep."

She kicked off her shoes and joined him on the sofa. "Flora Edwards was there."

"My former landlady at the Dixiana?"

"Yes, she's starting a campaign to get Dover changed back to Do Over. She says she wants to preserve our heritage."

"Might not be a bad thing."

"But think of the cost of renaming our town. Not just the sign on the highway, but the legal hoops we'd have to jump through. State. Federal. Not to mention Google searches."

Ethan chuckled. "You may have a point."

She reached over and took his hand. His heart skipped a beat for a few seconds.

"Thank you for watching Sadie. You'll make a great father one day."

He abruptly released her hand and stood. "I'm not cut out for the parenthood thing."

"What? Why do you say that?"

He was surprised to see disappointment cloud her blue eyes. But he had to make her understand. "I learned something from every foster home I was assigned. Sometimes I learned useful things, like handyman skills or minor car repairs. Other times it was how to mediate or when to keep my mouth shut. One thing I learned from every home I was in—I knew nothing about how families worked and I never would."

"But that doesn't mean you can't learn."

Ethan rubbed his jaw. How could he make her understand? "All I know is photography. I turned eight the day before my mom died. She'd given me a little camera. She left me alone for just a few minutes to run to the store a few blocks away. She never came back. A car hit her crossing the street. When Social Services showed up later that day, they wouldn't let me take anything with me but some clothes and my toothbrush. I hid the camera in my jacket and I managed to keep it with me. It became my shield, my protection against the outside world. It was the only way I knew how to live until that moment in Afghanistan." He inhaled a deep breath. "I'm still learning to live on the other side of the camera." He rose and headed to the door, willing himself not to look back at Nicki, but when she called his name, he turned. His gaze fell on her sweet face and the sadness in her eyes.

"I think you're wrong," she said. "You'd be a great father."

He wanted to believe her. But how did a man who'd never had a father know how to be one?

Nicki rested her hand on his arm. "Ethan, Sadie loves you."

Her words clogged his throat. "I love her, too. But

there's more to being a dad than liking kids." He took one last look into her troubled eyes, then left, reminding himself that Nicki had only one goal and it was to leave Dover.

Then he'd be alone again.

Nicki huddled deeper under the covers, trying to chase away the cold hollow in her heart left by Ethan's comments last night. While she could sympathize with his belief that his foster-care childhood had been a bad example of family life, that didn't mean he wouldn't make a good husband and father someday. She wanted to find a way to convince him that he was wrong. But she wasn't sure how.

Strange cries penetrated the lifting fog of sleep. Sadie was crying. Nicki forced her eyes open and glanced at the clock. She could have used another hour of sleep, but apparently Sadie had other ideas. Tossing off the covers, she swung her feet to the floor. Getting an early start wasn't a bad thing. There was still so much to do in the store. At least the tide had turned. She had to believe the weekend signaled a turnaround for Latimer's.

Tiptoeing into the nursery, she bent over the crib, smiling at her daughter. "Good morning, sweetheart." Her hand caressed the side of her baby's head. Her skin was dry and hot. "Sadie?" She reached to pick her up, but Sadie's arms began to shake. Her legs stiffened and her toes pointed downward.

"Sadie!" Fear exploded into panic as she watched her baby shake. "Ethan!" She turned and ran to the front door. He must have heard her scream because he was already in the hall when she opened it. "It's Sadie. She's shaking all over. I don't know what to do."

Ethan hurried to the crib. "We need to get her to the hospital. She's having convulsions."

Nicki's mind went numb. Blindly she followed Ethan's instructions, holding Sadie, who had finally stopped shaking, but lay quiet and still in her arms. In the backseat of her car, she kept one hand on Sadie's chest, praying for her to keep breathing.

"Where am I going, Nicki? Which way to the hospital?"

Her brain refused to cooperate. "Uh. Union Street. Follow it out to the highway and go toward Sawyer's Bend."

Her prayer became a hypnotic plea. Over and over she prayed for Sadie's life, begging God for mercy. Nicki was only vaguely aware of the drive to the hospital and of Ethan helping her into the E.R. Time passed in a haze. Insurance. Paperwork. Questions. All she knew was that Sadie was in her arms.

It wasn't until they were led into a small exam room that her mind began to clear. Ethan was at her side, his arm around her shoulders, muttering words of comfort.

The doctor finally entered and introduced herself as Dr. Wells. Nicki struggled to answer her questions.

"How long did the seizure last?"

Ethan's voice responded before Nicki could. "Minute and a half, maybe two. No longer."

Dr. Wells scooped Sadie up. "She's running a high fever. We're going to get that down, and then we'll examine her to see what's going on. We'll run a few tests." She started for the door. "Don't worry, Mrs. Collier. I'll take good care of little Sadie."

Nicki nodded, thinking how odd it was to hear her married name again. She'd stopped using it when she'd left her husband. The moment the door closed, Nicki's knees buckled. Ethan pulled her to him, wrapping his arms around her, resting his chin on the top of her head. She clung to him, unable to think.

Ethan eased her into the chair, keeping her hand in his. "What if it's something serious?" A surge of fear closed her throat, forcing her to gasp in a breath of air.

"Nicki, I think you should call your parents."

She balked at the suggestion. Her mom would probably blame her. She didn't need that now.

"Listen to me." He forced her to look at him. "I'm going to have to leave and get the store open soon. But I can't leave you here alone. Unless you want to close the store today. I'm sure the customers would understand."

"No. We're too close to turning things around. We have to open up." But she didn't want to call her mother.

"Nicki, honey, you need her at a time like this. Sadie's her granddaughter. She'd want to be here."

He was right. Slowly, she pulled her phone out of her purse. Before she could make the call, the door opened and a nurse looked in.

"Dr. Wells said Sadie's fever is coming down, but she wants to run a few tests."

Relief made Nicki light-headed. Burying her face in her hands, she muttered a thankful prayer then glanced at the nurse again. "My baby is going to be all right, isn't she?"

"We'll know more when the tests are completed."

The nurse left and Nicki dialed her parents' number with shaky fingers.

The sound of her mother's voice released the tears she'd been fighting. When her parents walked into the room a short while later, Nicki threw herself into her mother's arms. "Oh, Mom, I'm so scared."

"Tell me what happened."

Nicki explained and then they settled in to wait. Finally, the doctor entered the waiting room.

"Sadie is doing well. I don't think it was anything serious. Her fever spiked. It's not unusual in small children. When it happens so quickly, it can cause febrile seizures. A terrifying thing to witness, but not usually serious. I'd watch her for the next couple of days. She might be coming down with an infection or a cold. If she runs another fever, call your pediatrician right away."

"Can we take her home now?"

"Not yet. I'd like to get the test results back before we send her home. Are these your parents?"

Nicki made a quick introduction.

"Have any members of your family ever experienced these seizures?"

Nicki looked at her mother.

"No. Never. Why?"

"A child is more likely to have febrile seizures if either of his parents had them when they were young."

Dr. Wells looked at Ethan. "What about the father's family?"

Nicki crossed her arms over her chest, avoiding Ethan's glance. "The father is deceased. I don't know anything about his medical history."

"I see. Well. If you'll follow me, I'll take you to Sadie. You can stay with her until we get those test results."

She grabbed her purse and started from the room, followed closely by her parents. She glanced back at Ethan. He wasn't moving. There was something odd about his expression, but she didn't have time to think about that now. "Aren't you coming?"

"You go ahead. I'll open the store. Let me know as soon as you get the test results. I'll see you when you get home."

"Nichelle, come on," her mother said.

With one last glance at Ethan, Nicki followed her parents down the hall. The only thing on her mind now was getting to Sadie and seeing for herself she was all right.

By the time Ethan returned to Latimer's, he was emotionally drained and fighting a headache that squeezed his skull like a vise. The doctor had been encouraging about Sadie's condition, but he wouldn't be able to relax until he knew for sure. A traffic light blinked red, and he pulled to a stop. A knot of fear the size of a basketball lodged in the center of his chest. The memory of little Sadie in the throes of a seizure tore at his heart. She was so tiny, so fragile. Nicki's panic washed over him again. He hadn't known what to do either, but getting the sick baby to the hospital had seemed the most logical thing to do.

The light turned green, and he eased forward. He pulled the car to a stop near the back stairs of the store and dug out his cell, praying for some word from Nicki about Sadie.

Nothing.

He gripped the steering wheel tightly, giving it a frustrated shake. As he climbed from the car, his eyes automatically lifted to the spire visible above the buildings, and he offered up a heartfelt prayer for Nicki and the baby. Some of his fear eased, but his guilt lay like a pool of acid in his mind. He'd promised Nicki he would open the store. He'd make sure things went as planned today. It was the least he could do.

Inside the office, he put in the combination to the safe, removed the till and set it on the desk. How ironic. Nicki trusted him enough to give him a key to the store, and the combination to the safe, but he'd failed her on the most important thing in her life. He'd been so caught up in taking pictures, he'd missed that Sadie was getting sick. He hadn't learned a thing. Except to confirm what he'd always suspected. He'd make a lousy father.

Setting his jaw, he walked out to the register, counted out the coins and bills, then made a quick sweep of the store, straightening and making a mental note of items to be restocked. As he turned the Closed sign to Open, he hoped there wouldn't be any customers for a while. He needed time to process what had happened this morning.

He checked his phone again. No message from Nicki. Walking to the office, he stopped in the doorway, visions of Nicki and Sadie floating through his mind. This morning's scare had yanked the cover from his feelings, exposing the truth. He was in love with Nicki, and his heart belonged to little Sadie.

It was the last thing he needed right now. And he certainly wasn't qualified to be a part of their lives. And he couldn't forget Nicki's need to regain control of her life far away from Dover. He wasn't about to complicate her goal by confessing his feelings.

By lunchtime he'd still heard nothing from Nicki. He had to remind himself that she didn't owe him anything. She was with her family. The best thing for him to do would be to back off, rebuild the barrier around his heart and leave as soon as he could. Dover wasn't the haven he'd hoped for. Latimer's would be solvent soon, her dad back in charge. He'd hang in for the next week or so, then maybe head back to Atlanta.

His text alert tone sounded from his shirt pocket and he pulled out his cell. It was from Nicki.

Sadie fine. Waiting on last test result. Home in few hours.

The sense of relief left him shaky, but grateful. He wasn't sure how he'd avoid Nicki from now on when all he wanted to do was pull her into his arms and never let her go.

Nicki bundled Sadie close in her arms, rejoicing in the comfort of holding her. Her parents had driven her home from the hospital. They'd wanted to take her back to their house, but Nicki was craving some quiet time with her daughter and the comfort of her own apartment. "Mom, I'm going to go in the store first. I know Ethan will want to see for himself that Sadie is all right."

"I'll take your things upstairs. If you change your mind, we'll come and get you."

Warm affection filled her. Things had changed drastically in her relationship with her mother.

"Thanks, Mom, but all I want now is to be home."

Her mother touched her hair tenderly. "We'll call later to check on you. And please tell Ethan how much we appreciated his help today."

"I will." Nicki waved goodbye to her dad, who was waiting in the car, then went inside the store. She peeked first into the stockroom, then into the kitchen, but she didn't see Ethan. Which meant he must be waiting on customers. She saw him the moment she reached the sales floor.

"We're home."

Ethan searched her face, then looked at Sadie. "Is she all right?"

"She's fine." Emotion cracked her voice. Ethan's eyes

looked moist. "Would you like to see for yourself?" She started to hand Sadie to him, but he pulled back.

"No, no. I've got customers."

Puzzled, Nicki looked past him into the store, but didn't see any shoppers. Focusing her attention back on him, she noticed that his posture was rigid and his expression closed off. What was wrong with him? "Okay. I'm going upstairs to get Sadie settled in. Do you need me down here?"

"No. The store will be closing in an hour. I'll lock up."

"Thanks. Mom sent a casserole home with me for supper. I'll fill you in when you come over."

"Yeah. That's great. I'd better go check on the things." He held her gaze a moment, then walked away.

Disappointment crept into her throat. She'd envisioned a happy reunion, not the cool reception she'd just received. Searching her mind, she could find no reason for Ethan's behavior.

But when Ethan didn't show up for dinner an hour after the store closed, she crossed the hall and knocked on his door. For a moment, she thought he wasn't home. Finally he opened the door, but only partially, standing with one shoulder braced against the edge.

"Are you coming over? Sadie is about to fall asleep. I thought you'd want to say good-night." The torment in his dark eyes sparked her concern.

"I don't think so. I've got stuff to take care of tonight."

They'd been friends long enough for her to recognize when he was avoiding her. She wouldn't let him do this. "You have to eat. And if you don't want to eat, then come have some tea. I need to fill you in on Sadie.

I might need your help again, and I want you to be up to speed."

His shoulders relaxed and he inhaled slowly. "Fine." He stepped through the door and followed her across to her apartment. She noticed he was barefoot and wearing his favorite black sweatpants and white T-shirt that did little to hide his broad muscled chest.

"If you want to say good-night to Sadie, you'd better hurry. I'll fix you a glass of tea."

Ethan nodded and headed toward the nursery. Nicki's heart was tight with anxiety. She had no idea what was wrong with Ethan, but it scared her.

She fixed two glasses of tea, put a helping of the tuna casserole on a small plate and carried it to the coffee table in case he changed his mind about eating. Then she went to the nursery. Ethan was standing at the crib, gripping the rail and staring down at Sadie. He didn't look at her when she entered. She stepped beside him, resting her hand in the center of his back. She could feel the tension in his muscles. "She's fine, Ethan. She even smiled and jabbered on the way home."

He nodded, not taking his eyes off the sleeping child. "The tests?"

"All good."

"This is my fault."

"What?"

"Sadie being sick. I thought she felt warm when I put her to bed last night, but I thought it was the lights."

"Lights?"

He waved off the comment. "I should have told you. You would have known what to do."

"Ethan, you can't blame yourself for what happened. Her fever spiked. There's no way it was your fault. The good news is there was no underlying cause."

"I should have said something."

Nicki took his hand and tugged him to the living room. She crossed her arms over her chest and held his gaze. "You were the one who knew what to do, Ethan. I was too scared. I didn't do anything but scream. I didn't know whether to pick her up or leave her alone. You were the one who took charge, and I'll never be able to thank you for being there for me. For us."

Ethan stared over her head as if unwilling to accept her gratitude. He shook his head, but she reached up and took his face between her hands. "Stop. You cannot blame yourself for Sadie's fever. If anyone should feel guilty, it should be me. I'm her mother and I didn't see she was getting sick either. I checked her when I got home, but I missed it, too." A sudden lump of fear, guilt and gratitude clogged her throat, bringing tears to her eyes. "Things could have ended so differently."

Ethan pulled her into his embrace. "You're a wonderful mother. I won't let you think that way."

She slipped her arms around his waist. "And I won't let you blame yourself for something that wasn't your fault."

"I was supposed to be watching out for her."

"And you did. You got us to the hospital." She pulled away, quickly missing the warmth of his arms. "Come and sit down. I'll fill you in."

Reluctantly he joined her on the sofa, taking her hand in his and resting them both on his knee. "I told my mom how guilty I felt and she told me about an incident with my brother, Kyle, when he was playing soccer. He fell during the game and hurt his arm, but he got up and kept playing. Later that night Kyle started to complain and become feverish. They took him to the E.R. and found that the arm was broken. My mom felt awful. Said she should have known it was broken. She was his mother."

"And the point is?"

"That being a parent is a constant challenge. You do the best you can day by day."

"What if your best isn't good enough?"

"Then you put your trust in the Lord and He'll help you through. We can't do it alone."

At that moment she suddenly realized that she needed Ethan at her side as she raised Sadie. But how could she tell him? And what did this mean for her plans to leave Dover?

Chapter Eleven

Nicki glanced up as Ethan walked past her office door Friday, leaving a splinter in her heart when he didn't speak or glance her way. Nothing had been the same since Sadie's trip to the hospital. Ethan had built a barrier around himself, one that neither she nor Sadie could penetrate. He interacted only when necessary, and he hadn't visited with Sadie in two days. She missed the closeness they'd shared. She missed him.

Her gaze moved to the computer screen and the résumé she'd tweaked. It was time to start applying for the positions she'd targeted. Her dad was improving quickly, the store was on track to be in the black again, and she had saved up a small sum toward her move. She'd feel more confident if she had access to Brad's money, but her attorney was still working on that.

The prospect of leaving Dover didn't excite her the way it had a few weeks ago. She could think of only one reason why: Ethan. Frustrated, she left the office. Time on the floor helping customers was always a good way to keep her mind occupied. Unfortunately, the morning dragged on with few customers and little to do, raising her concerns for the store. She was straightening up the window display for the third time when a familiar voice called her name.

Nicki glanced up to see her father approaching. "Dad. What are you doing here?"

He gave her a quick hug. "I came to have lunch with my girls."

"I'd love that."

Ethan approached from the back corner of the store, where he'd been stocking merchandise. "Mr. Latimer." He shook his hand.

Nicki noticed he didn't smile or even attempt to make conversation. He was cool and detached. "Would you mind watching the store for a while? Dad wants to have lunch with me and Sadie."

"Sure. No problem."

Ethan walked away, leaving a knot of disappointment in her throat. Upstairs in her apartment, Nicki fixed sandwiches, placed them on the table, then reached for Sadie, but her father refused to relinquish the little girl.

"She's fine here on her granddaddy's lap."

"If you say so." They chatted a few minutes, enjoying their time together. Then Nicki sensed a change in her father's mood. One glance at the expression on his face told her she was in for a talking-to. The kind where he imparted advice whether she wanted it or not.

"So, what's going on between you and Ethan?"

"What do you mean?"

"Things seem strained between you."

No point in denying it. Her dad always figured things out. "He blames himself for not realizing Sadie was getting sick. I told him it wasn't his fault, but he's convinced he'd make a terrible father because he was raised in foster care."

"What do you think?"

"I know he'd be a good dad. Like you. He's kind, gentle, thoughtful. And he adores Sadie."

"So is that what you're looking for, then? A father for Sadie?"

"No. I mean…someday, but not now. I'm still planning on leaving Dover as soon as I can find a job. There's not much opportunity here."

Her father nodded thoughtfully. "Still determined to go it alone, huh? Nichelle, this independent trait of yours has always troubled me."

Nicki sighed. "I know."

"I'm beginning to think you have a limited understanding of what independence means."

"It means I'm a strong, capable woman able to control my own life."

"It can. And I'm so proud of your ability to conquer any obstacles in your way. After what you went through with Brad, it's understandable. But you're wrong if you think independence means you don't have to depend on anyone else. We all depend on someone. I depend on your mother. I depend on God every day. You depend on us—and Ethan. And Sadie depends on you."

"You don't think I can manage on my own?"

"I know you can, but could it be that your obsessive need to be on your own is more about your pride and insecurities than a real desire to move away just so you can prove yourself capable?" He reached over and took her hand in his. "Nichelle, real independence allows you to be who you are and pursue the things you love. Finding someone who gives you that kind of freedom is a special gift. Are you in love with him?"

"Maybe. I know there's something between us, and I care for him a great deal."

"You know that the man is in love with you?"

Nicki blushed. "You're wrong. I don't think he has any feelings for me beyond friendship." She remembered the times she'd thought he was going to kiss her and how disappointed she'd been when he hadn't. Did that spell love or simply mutual attraction?

Her father sighed. "Knowing you, you haven't made it easy for him. You probably reminded him every moment that you're leaving Dover ASAP and that you don't need anyone in your life. Am I right?"

"I guess."

Her father put his arm around her shoulders and gave her a hug. "Don't let your fears keep you from living your life. You deserve to be happy again." He smiled and waved goodbye.

Her father's words floated through her head the rest of the afternoon. Was she overcompensating with her need to be on her own? She couldn't deny that whenever thoughts of Brad surfaced, she was filled with a powerful need to show the world she wasn't that person anymore.

Her dad had raised another issue, as well. What exactly was the relationship between her and Ethan? She like being with Ethan. She liked talking to him, sharing Sadie's little milestones. Their celebration in the park the other night had filled her with a sense of completeness. Part of her wanted to explore a relationship with Ethan, to see where it would lead. But a part of her still craved a life away from her small hometown.

What did Ethan want? He'd said he'd come to Dover to decide on his future, but she doubted that included a woman with a child. Yet he adored Sadie and she knew he cared for her. But how much did he care?

He'd given her compliments, supported her at every turn, but he'd never kissed her. Was that why he kept pulling away at those moments? Had her fierce need to leave Dover prevented him from moving forward? The memory of his strength and comfort the night Sadie had gotten sick washed through her. He'd held her together when she was breaking into pieces. She'd needed him then and she was afraid she needed him now. He was always in her thoughts and her dreams. Pulling out her desk chair, she sat down.

A few months ago she'd had a clearly defined goal, but Sadie had changed everything, and Ethan had added another obstacle in her path. She'd thought she wanted a life free of restrictions, but lately she'd started to think about the importance of friends, family and heritage.

But she also had to be practical. She needed a job, and the prospects in Dover were slim. Obtaining a settlement from Brad's estate could take years. It was time to start sending out her résumés. She'd been waiting for the right moment. Well, it was here.

Her finger pressed the send button on her last résumé mailing right before the phone rang. When she hung up a few minutes later, her stomach churned, and a sob worked its way up her throat. Nicki scraped her hands through her hair. Just when she thought she had a handle on things, another obstacle popped up. Eyes burning with weariness, Nicki buried her face in her hands, praying fervently that this latest disaster wouldn't spell the end of Latimer's Office Supply.

"Nicki. Are you all right?"

The sound of Ethan's deep voice washed over her with warm comfort. Having someone to turn to when things got messy was a blessing she'd never expected to appreciate. Meeting Ethan's dark gaze, she was overcome with a deep need to step into his arms.

"The Hollis Company has canceled their account

with us. They're going to do business with Office Mart from now on."

Ethan hunkered down beside her office chair, resting one hand over hers. "Did they say why?"

She nodded, as tears slid down her cheeks. Ethan's kindness was her undoing. "They can offer better prices than we can. But we can't make it without them—their account covers our basic operating expenses. The rent and all the utilities."

Ethan squeezed her hand. "But with business picking up, maybe it won't be too big of a blow."

"No, it changes everything. Without Hollis, we're right back to where we were when you first came here. The increased business will keep us treading water, but it won't put the store back on its feet. If we lose any more accounts, we won't survive."

Ethan stood and took her hand, urging her to her feet. She knew she should remain professional, but she really needed a hug. Ethan pulled her close, wrapping her in strength and warmth and providing a solid anchor.

"We'll work this out. I know it's a blow, but don't give up."

"I can't let my dad lose his business. Maybe I was a fool to think a little reworking could make a difference. We need a huge infusion of cash, and even that might not work. I can't possibly offer the amount of merchandise and discounts the chain stores can. All I'm doing now is postponing the inevitable."

"You don't know that."

"I could offer reward cards or self-checkout."

Ethan tilted her face upward. "Those are good ideas, but I think you'd be smart to concentrate on what Latimer's does best. Customer service. Every day I hear how much the customers appreciate the one-on-one attention they receive here. Isn't that the bottom line of marketing, after all?"

She nodded. "I suppose."

"Don't give up yet. We'll get our heads together and come up with something."

"We?" Was he going to stand by her through this, too? "This isn't your problem, Ethan. I'm grateful for all you've done, but without the Hollis account, I might have to let you go."

Ethan pulled her closer. "That might not be so easy."

The intimate look in Ethan's eyes muddled her thoughts. "I can't ask you to stay."

He tilted his head. "I'd stay anyway. I promised you that I would be here for you. Nothing has happened to change that. I have a lot invested in this store. I'd like to see it back on its feet again."

"Why do you care?"

"Because the owner's daughter is an amazing, determined, beautiful, caring woman and I like working alongside her." Ethan shifted slightly, his palms cradling her face, and his thumbs gently brushed over her damp cheeks. He lowered his head. Nicki held her breath, anticipating the moment she'd thought about for weeks.

His kiss was gentle, questioning, as if gauging her response. She melted into him, giving herself over to the sensation. He deepened the kiss, stealing the strength from her knees. She held on to his shoulders, grateful for his arm around her waist, the only thing holding her upright.

He pulled her closer, his heart beating fiercely against hers. He ended the kiss, taking her shoulders in his hands. She heard him mutter something, but couldn't make sense of it.

When she opened her eyes, he was gone. Sinking

into her desk chair, she tried to sort out her tangled emotions. The kiss had satisfied her curiosity and ripped the cover off her feelings. She was in love with Ethan Stone. For the first time, she found herself wondering what staying in town might offer.

Nicki dusted the electronics display, wiped the devices free of fingerprints, then stood back to scan the aisle. She liked keeping things neat and tidy. She liked even better that restocking the shelves had become a frequent task. The sidewalk sale had infused new life into Latimer's. Unfortunately, the departure of Hollis had plunged the store back into survival mode. The store could limp along for a while, but she didn't want to hand a struggling business back to her father when he returned to work.

But Latimer's wasn't the main thing on her mind now. Her love for Ethan was. What to do about it had kept her restless all night. The jingling doorbell drew her to the end of the aisle to greet her customer. Maybe they were here to look at the new electronics display. She'd been encouraged by the number of sales so far. Cassidy had spread the word about the cute cell-phone covers and Nicki had reordered three times.

The smile on her face faded a bit when she saw a woman she didn't recognize. Tall and slender, her willowy frame was sheathed in a perfectly tailored navy dress that screamed business yet somehow reminded everyone she was a woman. She wore her dark hair short and slightly spiky on top. It was a style no one in Dover would ever adopt. Her high heels sounded an unfamiliar tattoo as she walked across the old wood floors.

Nicki was suddenly aware of her five-foot-four height, the baby weight she'd yet to shed and the plain tan slacks and simple pink blouse she wore. Scolding herself for making comparisons, she forced her smile up a notch. "Welcome to Latimer's. Can I help you?"

The woman's dark eyes scanned the store and Nicki could read the disdain in her posture. "I need to speak to the manager."

"That would be me. Nicki Latimer. How can I help?"

The woman made a quick and dismissive assessment of her before lifting her chin. "I need to see Ethan Stone."

A cold chill seeped into Nicki's veins. "He's not here at the moment. If you'd like to leave a message, I'll tell him you're in town."

"No. I don't think so. It's important that I see him. Where does he live?"

"He has an apartment above the store," Nicki said, immediately regretting she'd shared that fact with this stranger.

The woman scanned her again. "Convenient. I'll wait for him there."

"I couldn't let you into his apartment without his permission." The woman's attitude scrubbed the warmth from her tone.

The woman took a step closer. "Oh, he won't mind. I'm Karen Holt. We're good friends."

Her implication was clear. Was she an old girlfriend? Wife? Ethan hadn't talked about anyone, certainly not a spouse. Nicki fought to keep a smile on her face. "I think I'd better call him. I'm his landlord as well as his employer, and I have a responsibility to protect his privacy." She slid her phone from her pocket and dialed. It went to voice mail. Now what? The store would be closing in a few minutes. If this woman was someone important to Ethan and she turned her away, he might be upset. Nicki glanced at the clock. He should be back in fifteen minutes or so. He'd run to Durrant's Hardware for lightbulbs. What could happen in that length of time?

She met the woman's gaze as she saw triumph in her eyes. Nicki didn't like feeling defeated. It was too reminiscent of the life she'd escaped. But she didn't want to upset Ethan either. She faced the woman again. "Well, if you'll give me a few moments to close up, I'll take you upstairs."

Nicki locked the front door and flipped the sign to Closed. She would close out the register when she came back downstairs. Lifting Sadie from her crib, Nicki grabbed the keys and stepped out into the store again. "Follow me please, and I'll let you into his place."

Waves of disdain washed from the unpleasant woman as Nicki led the way up the exterior stairs to the second floor. At the door to Ethan's apartment, the woman huffed. "Quaint."

Nicki pursed her lips. She'd like nothing better right now than to pinch the nose right off the woman's perfectly-made-up face. She unlocked the door and stepped back. Karen stepped inside Ethan's small apartment, keeping her arms close to her sides as if afraid to touch anything.

Nicki slipped the key into her pocket. "I'll keep trying to reach him."

"You do that."

Downstairs, Nicki secured Sadie in her carrier and took her out to the front counter so they could visit while she counted the till and prepared the bank slip.

"I don't know who she thinks she is, but I do not like her." But what if Ethan did? Was this the kind of woman he preferred? Polished, sophisticated? What did it matter? But the thought of Ethan and that woman left her cold and oddly hurting inside.

Karen Holt knew things about Ethan Nicki didn't. Like his past. Nicki no longer worried about the blanks on Ethan's application. He'd filled in most of them for her. But there was still a lot she didn't know and she wanted to know everything.

"It's none of our business, is it, sweetie?" Gathering up Sadie, Nicki secured the store and started up the outside stairs. She was turning the lock in the exterior door when Ethan pulled up. He waved and hurried to join her. His gaze caressed her face, then slid to Sadie.

"All closed up for the night?"

She nodded and stepped into the hallway. Ethan reached out for Sadie, holding her securely against his chest and smiling. The sight created a warm rush in her chest. The tenderness this big man displayed gently holding the tiny baby touched her heart in a way she'd never felt before.

Nicki looked into his eyes. "You have company. A woman. Karen Holt."

Ethan's dark eyes narrowed, and the muscle in his jaw tightened. "Where is she?"

"In your apartment. She said you were old friends. She asked to wait in your place. I didn't think you'd mind."

"We are not friends. Karen is a cold, grasping..." He looked her in the eyes. "She's not my friend." She thought he was going to say something else, but he pressed his lips together and took her upper arm in his hand, steering her toward her apartment.

"I'm sorry. I should have made her come back later."

The anger in Ethan's eyes faded and they grew tender. "No. You did the right thing."

Sadie began to fuss and squirm. "I think our little lady must be hungry." He placed a kiss on Sadie's temple before handing her back. He smiled at Nicki. "I'd better go deal with Karen."

She nodded, stepping into her apartment and closing the door. He'd said "our little lady." A smile spread over her face. She realized she'd like nothing better than to be his. Forever.

Now she only had to convince Ethan that they belonged together.

Ethan waited until Nicki was inside her apartment before entering his own. Karen was seated at his desk, using his laptop. His blood boiled. He stalked to the desk, slamming the lid closed. "What are you doing here?"

Karen jerked her hands away. "You could have taken off a finger. Hello to you, too." She spun in the chair and smiled up at him. "You're looking good, Ethan. I didn't think small-town life would appeal to you."

"What do you want?"

"To see you." She stood. "You've been avoiding me. Changing phones. Not returning calls. I get concerned when my people go missing."

"I told you I was taking a leave of absence. I also remember telling you I'd contact you when I was ready. I'm *not* ready."

"But I am. There are places in turmoil, Ethan. Places I need to send you to capture the images of conflict the way only you can."

Ethan fought the urge to toss her out. "I'm not going back to that. I told you I'm done taking pictures."

"Oh? Then what are those photos I saw on your laptop scrolling across the screen? Your new employer and her kid. You must have a camera here someplace."

"Cell phone. It's not the same thing."

"The point is, you're still compelled to take pictures. You can't help it. It's in your blood. Canon, Nikon, point-and-shoot or cell, it doesn't matter. That's why I want you back. You've hidden out in this backwater long enough. Time to come back to Atlanta and go to work."

"I like it here. I might stay permanently. If you won't give me the time I need, then I'll hand in my resignation here and now."

Karen crossed her arms. "I refuse to accept it."

"You can't force me to leave."

"No. But I can make you *want* to leave, given a big enough incentive. Like a Pulitzer."

Ethan rested his hands on his hips. He'd won many awards for his photography. Several prestigious ones in the field. But he'd never considered the Pulitzer Prize. "You've lost touch with reality, Karen."

"What if I told you it's already been submitted for consideration?"

Ethan narrowed his gaze. The smug look on Karen's face told him she wasn't bluffing. "How is that possible? I haven't even sent you my last photo file."

Karen's grin widened. "Well, actually, you did. When you were in the hospital in Atlanta recuperating from your wounds, they called me to come and collect your things. I'm listed as your emergency contact, remember? So I got your camera and processed the files."

"You had no right." Nausea pooled in his gut at the thought of Karen taking his things and the fact that she'd published his photos without his approval.

"Oh, but I do. Check your contract. The network owns your work. Not you."

Ethan took a step closer to his boss. "There are certain pictures in those files that should never be seen."

She smiled and opened his laptop again. "You mean like this one?" She tapped the keys and the image of the mother and child filled the screen.

Ethan looked away. He should have deleted the picture. He wasn't sure why he hadn't. "You can't publish that."

"Everyone should see that picture. It'll put your name on the map. It'll lift TNZ to the top of the chain."

Ethan ran his hands through his hair. He couldn't let her do it. He couldn't let others see the horror he had. Especially Nicki. What would she think of him after seeing that? "Don't do this."

"Why? Are you so smitten with your little store manager and her kid that you'd throw away a chance at a Pulitzer? I don't think so. You win that and you can do whatever you want with your career." She turned and tapped a few more keys, bringing up a picture of Nicki and Sadie. His heart skipped a beat. Nicki's love for her child was evident in her eyes, the glow on her skin and the way she held the baby.

Karen looked back at him. "Even with a cell-phone camera, you can't help but capture true emotions. Think about it. It's always been you and your camera. Nothing else fits into your life, Ethan. Nothing else defines you."

Karen stood, picked up her purse and walked to the door, stopping at the threshold to smile at him. "And what will you do for a living? Work here? Filling shelves for minimum wage? I know you think you're in love with her, but you know you're not cut out to be a family man. Raising kids, mowing grass, church on Sunday."

"Stop."

"I know you, Ethan. You're a famous, well-respected

photographer. You like nice things. You like good food and fine wine and travel. You won't last six months in this one-horse town."

Ethan heard the door close behind Karen, his thoughts slamming back and forth like a screen door in the wind. Karen was right. He'd worked his entire life to reach the top of his profession. His camera was all he'd known since his mother had died. She was also right that he was poorly equipped to stand in the place of husband and father to Nicki and Sadie.

But he'd changed. He wanted more than the life he'd had. He wanted roots, permanence. A home and family, and he wanted it with Nicki. The kiss he'd shared with Nicki had rocked his foundation and shown him how deeply he cared. Holding her, kissing her had been like finding a home, the place he'd searched for his whole life. The emotions were powerful, overwhelming, yet he'd experienced no fear, no doubt. He'd feared he was unable to let her into his heart, only to find she was already there.

For a brief moment, he'd seen something in her eyes that had given him hope that she cared for him too, but it had been replaced quickly with a shadow of doubt, leaving him confused and convinced that Nicki wasn't looking for a romantic entanglement.

Karen had seen his feelings for Nicki. They were clearly revealed in every photo he'd taken. But he couldn't tell Nicki. She had dreams she was determined to achieve. Dreams that didn't include him.

His gaze drifted to the closet that held his equipment. What if he went back to Atlanta? He could refuse any assignments in conflict areas. Could he do it? There'd been a time not too long ago when he'd doubted he'd ever touch a camera again. Sadie had helped him over that hurdle. But taking pictures of someone he loved was much different from taking pictures for a living.

Right now he needed to talk to Nicki and explain. He needed to come clean about everything that had happened to him, and maybe she could help him reach a decision. Maybe he should tell her how he felt, let her know how much she'd come to mean to him.

No. Not yet. Maybe when the store was on course and she was free from her obligations to her parents. For the time being, he prayed he'd be able to keep his feelings hidden.

Chapter Twelve

Nicki patted Sadie's back gently and was rewarded with a tiny burp. "That feels better, doesn't it, pumpkin?" She wiped her little mouth and placed a kiss on her soft cheek. If she could get her to sleep at a decent time, Nicki planned on watching her favorite TV show and going to bed early. Though after her encounter with Karen Holt, she doubted she'd be able to concentrate or sleep.

Who was she and what was she to Ethan? She scolded herself mentally. It didn't matter because it was none of her business. What she needed was a long talk with Debi. Looking around for her cell phone, she realized she'd left it on her desk downstairs in the store.

Grabbing up her keys, she opened the apartment door. Angry voices brought her to a halt. Karen and Ethan. She froze, trying not to listen to their conversation, but it was impossible given they were only a few feet away across the narrow hall.

"—you're in love with her, but you know you're not cut out to be a family man. Raising kids, mowing grass, church on Sunday."

"Stop."

"I know you, Ethan. You're a famous, well-respected photographer. You like nice things. You like good food and fine wine and travel. You won't last six months in this one-horse town."

The more she heard, the more Nicki wanted to slink away in the shadows. Finally the woman stalked off and Ethan slammed his door shut. Nicki quietly closed her own door, her heart beating triple time as she tried to sort through what she'd heard. Was it true? Was Ethan in love with her?

The idea brought a rush of heat to her cheeks. She laid Sadie under her gym, then paced the room. That woman seemed to think so. And so did her father. Yes, there were sparks between them, an electric awareness of each other whenever they were close, and the kiss had suggested he cared a great deal.

The woman had also reminded Ethan he wasn't cut out for family life, something he believed, as well. But they were both wrong. She'd seen his gentleness with Sadie and his delight in the little things she would do. She'd experienced firsthand his strength and support, the way he watched over her, with a quiet protectiveness. Ethan was the perfect family man.

She carried Sadie into her room, prepared her for bed and then settled into the rocker, feeding her. The woman had said Ethan was famous, important, and that he liked nice things, and he'd be bored quickly in Dover. Was he longing to return to his former life? From everything he'd said to her, he had no desire to be a photographer anymore.

Nicki tucked Sadie into bed, then curled up on the sofa, hugging a pillow to her chest. Somehow Ethan had captured her heart. If he left, she wasn't sure she could ever fill the void he'd leave in her life.

* * *

Ethan knocked on the door to Nicki's apartment, rubbing the back of his neck as he sorted through the things he needed to say. She'd have questions, and he'd put this talk off for way too long. The door opened and he looked into her eyes, surprised to find them filled with sadness.

"We need to talk."

"No need. Your private life is none of my business."

"But I want to tell you about it."

Nicki hesitated a moment, then stepped aside to let him enter.

"Is Sadie in bed?"

"I just put her down. Did you have a nice visit with your…friend?"

Ethan was hurt that Nicki didn't suggest he go and see the baby. "She's my boss. But I've taken a leave from the network."

"So. You're some kind of famous photographer." He raised his eyebrow in a question. She shrugged. "You know how voices carry in this old building."

He'd wondered how much she'd heard. "I told you that."

"You said you were a photographer. Not that you were famous."

"I'm not." He dragged his hand across his chin. "There are some things I haven't told you that I want you to understand."

"Fine." She sat down at the far end of the sofa.

Ethan relaxed a little. At least she was giving him the opportunity to explain. He sat on the edge of the sofa, bracing his elbows on his knees.

"I've told you how I became a photographer and how I've been an observer of life and not a participant. That ability served me well for most of my life. After college I went to work for TNZ News and eventually ended up embedded with the troops in the Middle East. But the last year things were getting tough. One day I was taking pictures in a market. I'd just focused in on a mother and infant when the place exploded. I kept shooting and caught the image of the mother and child…on the ground…"

Nicki uttered a soft gasp, but he couldn't look at her. "Afterward, I couldn't process what I was seeing. It killed something in me. The next explosion knocked me out. I woke up in the hospital, knowing I'd never pick up a camera again." He inhaled slowly, knowing he had to face Nicki. What would he see in her eyes?

Before he could look at her, she reached out and traced the scar beside his mouth.

"I'm so sorry you had to see something so horrible."

Her touch gave him the courage to continue. "The doctors called it cumulative stress disorder. A buildup of emotional events that finally overwhelm you. Guess I spent one too many years in the combat zone."

"So why was that woman here?"

"She wants me to go back to work. But I'm not sure I'll stay with the news agency. That's why I came here. I wanted to find a new life, to learn to live in the moment and not through my pictures."

"Have you? Learned?"

He smiled, reaching out and touching her cheek. "You've taught me. You are never out of the moment— you wear your emotions like a banner, never afraid, never holding back. That first day you had me wait on customers, I was lost. But then I thought about how you handled the people who came to the store, and I just copied what you did."

"So, what now? Did your boss come all this way just to ask you to come back to work?"

Ethan stood and moved to the window. "She got hold of the photos from my last assignment and submitted one to the Pulitzer Prize committee."

"Ethan, that's wonderful. Think what that would mean to your career."

He turned to face her. "I don't want to stay in this field. Besides, the picture she submitted is the one that destroyed me. If it could break me, think what it might do to others who will see it."

Nicki came to his side. "But what if it could help them understand? Maybe you should share it."

Ethan shook his head. She had no idea what she was suggesting.

"Maybe you need to face that moment before you can move on with your life."

"No. I'm in a good place now. I've got a job I like, a group to support me. I've got…you and Sadie."

Nicki set her hands on her hips. "Show me the pictures, Ethan. I want to see them. I'm a big girl. I've seen pictures of the Holocaust, images from wars. Use me as a gauge to see how others might react. Let me share the pain with you. Maybe together we can find a way to conquer it."

Was she right? Would having her at his side give him a perspective he lacked? She hadn't turned away when she'd learned he suffered from PTSD. Maybe she was strong enough to face this, too.

"Go. Get your computer."

When he returned, he placed the laptop on the kitchen table, opened the photo file and selected the first image. Nicki gently moved him aside and sat down. One by one she scrolled through the images of war. Ethan's gut knotted tighter as each image passed across the screen. He couldn't read her reaction. His heartbeat quickened as she neared the end and the last two images he'd captured.

She paused a long time on the shot of the mother and child, happy and smiling in the marketplace. He closed his eyes. Not wanting to see the next photograph. He heard her gasp. He opened his eyes. Nicki had her hands to her face. She started to cry. He kicked himself for listening to her and letting her see the horror that haunted him. He reached across to kill the screen, but she stopped him with her hand.

"Don't."

She looked up at him, the tears in her eyes like a knife in his heart. "I'm sorry."

She shook her head and slipped her arms around his waist, resting her head against his shoulder. He held her close, the embrace filling him with a comfort and peace he'd never known, yet had secretly ached for his entire life.

She held him for a moment, then eased out of the embrace and raised her hands to his face. "Now I understand why you reacted the way you did when you saw Sadie the first time. We must have been in the same pose as the mother and child you photographed."

He nodded, unable to find his voice. "I was going to quit that afternoon."

"Why didn't you?"

"I found you crying. You told me about the problems with the store, and I thought about the robberies. I couldn't leave you and Sadie alone."

"I'm glad you stayed, Ethan. I couldn't have endured these last few weeks without you."

He shook his head. "You'd have done fine without me."

She held his gaze. "That's the problem. I'm not sure I could have."

He smiled. "Miss Independent?"

"Maybe I'm not so independent after all. I like having you around."

Her hand touched the side of his face. He looked into her blue eyes, wanting to believe what he saw there. He told himself to pull back, but it was hopeless. He drew her close. There was no turning back now.

Ethan took her hands from his face, kissed each palm, then repositioned them on his shoulders. "I like being around." He lowered his head and captured her mouth. The kiss ignited a depth of love he hadn't known he possessed. When he ended the kiss, he saw his own emotions reflected in her eyes. Pulling her close again, he held her against his chest, totally in the moment. He didn't need a picture. He'd remember this for the rest of his life.

Nicki traced the condensation on her glass of sweet tea, darting glances toward the door of the Camellia Tea Room. She'd called Debi early this morning to schedule some girl talk over lunch. She needed another perspective on things. Especially after the news she'd received this morning, which had further complicated her life.

She brushed her bangs off her forehead, remembering the way Ethan had done the same the other night, his fingers grazing her skin before he had kissed her. The kiss had rocked her, left her longing for confirmation of his feelings. But it hadn't come.

Yesterday they'd attended church together, then had dinner with her folks. Later they'd taken a lovely walk in the park. Yet, when he'd said good-night, he'd only smiled and brushed a gentle hand against her cheek, leaving her confused and off balance again. She was in love with him, but she was confused about what to do about it. He was a man she could spend her life with. A husband for her, a friend and partner, and a wonderful father for Sadie. But she had no idea if Ethan felt the same. When he looked at her with those warm chocolate eyes, filled with affection, she believed he cared. What he said, or rather didn't say, was different.

Even those heart-stopping kisses had come at times when they were both needing comfort and reassurance. Maybe that was all he'd intended them to be. So had she imagined the emotion in his last kiss?

Nicki glanced up to see her friend walk in and waved. Nicki had chosen a table in the back so they could talk privately.

Debi slid into the chair and leaned forward, her expression reflecting her concern. "What's going on? You never call in the morning."

Nicki chewed her lip. "I don't know where to start. I need help sorting things out. I've tried, but I keep going around in circles. You've got to help me."

"It's Ethan, isn't it?"

Nicki coughed when her swallow of tea went down wrong. "Why do you think that?"

"What else could it be? How's Sadie doing?"

"She's fine. Mom is watching her today."

Debi gave her a knowing glance. "It's nice having grandparents in town to help out."

Nicki nodded. "I have to admit it makes working at the store easier. Since Sadie was sick, we've all become closer." She took a deep breath. "I got a job offer this morning. A great position with a marketing firm in Branson, Missouri."

"Are you going to take it?"

"I don't know. I should be thrilled. It's more than I'd hoped for, but I'm starting to see that striking out on our own is going to be harder than I imagined."

"And where does Ethan fit into this? And don't tell me you don't love him, because I know better."

"Even if I do, I'm not sure he feels the same way. Sometimes he acts like he cares, but he's never said the words."

"Have you told him how you feel?"

"No. Well, I've dropped some hints."

"Hints? Nicki. You can't hint to a man. You have to say it straight-out. Has he kissed you?"

Nicki hesitated. "Yes."

"More than once?"

"Yes, but I can't throw away a job that will give Sadie and I a solid future over a few kisses."

Debi shook her head and frowned. "This isn't about the job. It's about you being afraid to risk loving again. Nicki, Ethan is nothing like Brad."

After telling her parents about her life with Brad, Nicki had confided in her friend, as well. "I know but—"

"Nicki, hasn't he proved himself every day? He's worked alongside you to save the store. He fixed up that apartment for you. He loves that baby, and he would never dominate you. He's content to let you shine. He's the only person I know who actually likes that independent streak of yours."

Nicki absently turned her fork over and over. Debi had a point. Ethan was all Debi said, but none of that mattered if he didn't have any feelings for her. "But I've only known Ethan a few weeks."

"And no one had a chance to know Brad at all. Maybe if we had we could have warned you away. You planned that destination wedding in Saint Thomas in only a few days, with only your parents and me as guests, then jetted off to Europe on your honeymoon that same day. It was a very rushed affair. I had a bad feeling from the start about you two."

"That was Brad's idea. I thought the impromptu wedding was so romantic. I should have seen that it was a prelude of what was to come."

Debi patted her hand. "It's done. You have another chance with a great guy. If you ask me, I think you should tell him about the job offer and see how he reacts. Maybe he'll ask you to stay, or maybe he'll go with you. But the first thing you have to decide is what it is you really want."

What did she want? Branson would be a dream come true. The salary was generous, and she'd welcome living in a larger city again. But she'd be sacrificing her parents, old friends, roots. And maybe a father for her little girl?

Nicki chewed her bottom lip. She was right back where she'd started. How did she choose between independence and roots? Until she knew how Ethan felt, she was mired in a pool of indecision and questions.

Ethan stretched his legs out, resting his feet on the ottoman in Nicki's living room. She'd invited him for supper. Their relationship had turned a corner in the past few days. There was a new closeness between them. He was hopeful that Nicki had developed feelings for him. But while he was certain she enjoyed his company, she'd given no indication that she might be changing her mind about leaving Dover. He'd considered coming clean and telling her how he felt, but he'd never wanted to pressure her with a relationship she'd never asked for.

He'd watched Sadie again last night for a short time

while Nicki had gone to the grocery store. He'd resisted, but she'd been determined to show him that he could babysit without anything horrible happening. Watching the baby again had chased away his lingering anxiety and much of his guilt.

It had been a good week. He'd taken his camera to her parents' on Sunday and captured as many moments as possible. He'd decided to start a photo album for Nicki. And himself. When it came time to leave, he'd have plenty of shots to remember his time in Dover.

Nicki came into the living room, a sweet smile on her face as she curled up beside him on the sofa.

"Is she asleep?"

She nodded. "She looks so beautiful when she sleeps."

"She looks like you." Ethan reached up and touched a finger to her hair, letting the soft golden strands feather across his skin. She shifted closer, her hand resting against his jaw.

"You've become very important to me, you know."

"Have I?"

She nodded. "Ethan, I think I may be changing my mind about some things."

His breath caught in his chest. "What's that?"

"Everything. Dover. You and me." She lowered her hand and sighed as if uncertain of how to proceed.

Ethan's hope soared. Maybe now was the time. The opening he'd been waiting for. It was risky, but if she felt the way he did, and he didn't tell her, he could lose her forever. He caressed her cheek with his palm, thrilled at the softness and the way she looked at him.

"Nicki, there's something I need to say to you."

She met his gaze, her blue eyes turning dark and troubled. "Let me go first." She took a deep breath. "I've been offered a job in Missouri."

His chest contracted, squeezing out all the air. "I see." His voice sounded odd to his ears.

She nodded, holding his gaze as if waiting for something. He wanted to tell her to turn it down. To stay with him in Dover, but he wouldn't do that. Nicki didn't like to be told what to do. He cleared his throat. "Is it a good offer?"

Nicki lowered her lashes and looked away. "Yes. Better than I expected. I wanted to know what—"

Her cell phone rang, shattering the mood. She hesitated a moment, then rose and went to the kitchen table to pick it up. She glanced at the screen, exhaling a small gasp before answering.

Concerned, Ethan stood and moved closer, praying it wasn't bad news.

"Hello. Yes." She stilled a moment, listening intently as she paced the small kitchen. "I can't believe this. I never expected it to happen. How much?" Her hand went to her mouth. "Yes. I will. Okay. Thank you. Thank you for everything."

The startled look on her face filled him with alarm. "Is everything all right?"

Slowly she smiled and nodded, placing her hands on her cheeks. "That was my attorney. She's reached a settlement with Brad's estate. Twice the amount I'd hoped for. I can't believe it. It's all coming together. In a few weeks Dad will be back at work, and Sadie and I can finally start over." She threw her arms about his neck and held on tight.

He held her close as his heart shattered into tiny pieces inside his chest. Her dream had been realized. There was no way he could tell her now. What he felt didn't matter. All that mattered was that Nicki was happy.

He set her away from him, unable to endure the closeness any longer.

"Well, now you have everything you wanted." He turned to go, wanting to put as much distance as possible between them.

"Ethan, wait. We weren't finished talking, were we?"

"It's not important." He cradled her face between his hands and kissed her lips softly. "Good night."

Nicki had everything she needed to start a new life elsewhere, which meant his days in Dover were coming to an end. Without them here, there was no reason to stay. Though how he'd live without them, he had no idea.

Chapter Thirteen

Nicki bit her bottom lip, marveling at how phone calls could drastically change a person's life. When she'd taken over the store, each phone call had brought a new problem to solve. This week, the phone calls had all been answers to her prayers.

Her first impulse was to run to Ethan with the good news. For a moment last night she'd thought he was going to tell her he loved her, but after the call from her attorney, he'd shut down. She could draw only one conclusion. His feelings for her were merely those of friendship. Nothing more. Her heart ached. She'd fallen in love with a man who didn't want her.

Still, she owed him the courtesy of sharing the news. He'd been the one to encourage her to focus on customer service, after all, but first she needed to call her father. Ethan was removing a shipping label from a large carton when she entered the stockroom.

"Guess what?"

He glanced over his shoulder before standing. "What?"

"Mr. Hollis just called. He's decided to start doing all his business with Latimer's again."

"Did he say why?"

She nodded, looking for a smile in the brown eyes, but they were devoid of any emotion. "He said he never appreciated our personal customer service until he left. He said it was worth the extra expense to know his orders would be handled by people of integrity who cared about his business as much as he did." She stilled, anticipating a hug from Ethan, but he kept his distance.

"Good customer service to the rescue."

"And a good plan B."

Ethan shrugged off the comment. "Have you told your dad?"

She nodded. "He's thrilled and eager to get back to work. Mom's decided to help him, so things should be okay soon."

"That's good."

He held her gaze a brief moment, almost as if he were memorizing her face. The space between them grew tense and awkward, something she'd never experienced with him before. She started to reach out to him, to try to talk, but he turned away, leaving a cold, aching hole in her heart.

Nicki gripped the steering wheel, fighting to stay within the speed limit as she made her way to Debi's house. She'd gone to her parents' after work and had just finished feeding Sadie when her father had told her the thieves targeting downtown stores had been captured. Her relief had quickly changed to fear when he'd told her the police officer who'd made the arrest had been shot. It was Jerry Gordon.

A quick call to her friend had assured her that Jerry had suffered only a minor wound and was already home from hospital, but knowing Debi's feelings about her husband's job, Nicki had decided an in-person visit was called for. Debi was waiting on the front porch when Nicki arrived. After exchanging hugs, they went inside. "How's Jerry?"

"I'm fine." He strode past them with a tired smile on his face and his left arm in a sling. "Everyone is making a big deal out of this. The important thing is we caught the guys."

Nicki gave Jerry a hug too, then took the glass of iced tea Debi offered her. "So who were they?"

"Some guys from up in Jackson. We don't have all the details yet, but I have a feeling there's more behind this. We'll just have to wait and see." Jerry rubbed his arm. "Think I'll go lie down for a bit."

The moment he was out of sight, Debi exhaled a heavy sigh as the two women sat down. "My worst nightmare."

"I can't even imagine. How are you holding up?"

"Actually, I'm good. It's almost like the fear is less now. I think I've come to terms with the risk. Jerry loves his job, he feels he's been called to do this, and he's happier than I've ever seen him. I've turned Jerry and his job over to God, and I know whatever happens, He'll see us through."

"I don't know if I could be that strong."

"Nicki, you already are strong. Look what you've been through, and you're still here and stronger for it." She took a deep breath. "Nick, I learned something else, too. We never know when our time is up. We need to make the most of our opportunities while we have them. Jerry and I aren't going to waste a moment from here on, and I don't want you to either."

"What do you mean?"

"I think you should tell Ethan that you love him before it's too late. Stop waiting for him to say something first. He's a man. They aren't good at expressing their feelings."

"I don't know." What if he rejected her?

"Do you want to wake up ten years from now alone, watching Sadie grow up without a father because you were too afraid to risk your heart?"

Nicki wasn't ready to deal with this now. She rose and headed for the door, giving the excuse that she needed to get back to Sadie, who was still at her parents'.

Debi walked her to the door. "Nick, why aren't you active in church anymore? You used to be involved in several ministries, but now you only attend the Sunday service."

A guilty conscience kept her from looking directly at her friend. "I will, once I get my life on track and get the store on its feet."

Debi touched her arm. "Don't you have that backward? Shouldn't you be looking to God first and let Him work on the rest?"

Nicki mulled over Debi's advice on the drive back to her parents. She put God first. Every morning since moving into the apartment she made sure she had devotional time so she could start the day with scripture. Sitting in church, however, was a different matter.

Seeking a distraction from her troubling thoughts, she turned on the radio.

Suddenly a horn honked from the car behind her and she realized the light had turned green and she hadn't moved. Turning into her parents' driveway, she stared blindly out the windshield. She was uncomfortable in church because she didn't think God would welcome her back. Brad had hated religion, so she'd set her faith aside to appease him. Her shameful behavior had placed a barrier between her and God. Was she trying to earn

God's love, too? God had protected her and brought her home, but instead of letting Him take her shame and toss it to the ends of the earth, she'd hidden behind it, afraid to face Him.

But God loved her even more than her parents did. If her earthly father had welcomed her back freely, why had she doubted her heavenly Father would do the same?

With her head in her hands, she prayed. "Father, forgive me. I've been a stupid, silly child."

Something was wrong.

Ethan pushed back from his small desk and walked to the window that looked out onto the gravel parking area below. It was dark; only the glow of the floodlight illuminated the parking lot. It was late, after ten. Nicki and Sadie had come home hours ago, but he'd resisted the urge to check on them.

The distant wail of a siren brought his gaze back to the window. Another siren rose, this one closer. Glancing sideways, he peered at the odd yellow glow coming from the store down the block. Raising the window, he leaned out, inhaling the acrid smell of fire. The sirens grew louder. A bright green fire truck, lights flashing, pulled to a stop in the lot down the way. Flames erupted from the roof two buildings down. The one where Nicki's friend Debi worked.

Adrenaline coursed through his veins. The buildings were old and shared common walls. The flames could spread in minutes. It was dangerous to stay here. Yanking open the door, he dashed across the hall and pounded on Nicki's. "Nicki, wake up. There's a fire." He pounded louder. "Nicki!"

He was about to break the door down when she appeared.

"What's wrong?"

He pushed past her, nearly knocking her down. "The insurance building is on fire. I've got to get you and Sadie out of here." She froze. Her eyes widened in fear. "Go get dressed. I'll get the baby. Hurry."

He hurried into the nursery and grabbed the diaper bag. Sadie was sleeping soundly, but he had to wake her and get her and her mother safely out and away. Scooping the tiny child into his arms, he cradled her close to his chest, covering her lightly with a blanket. He met Nicki in the hall. He steered her ahead of him out the door and down the hall to the back stairs.

She emitted a cry of alarm when she saw the glow and smelled the smoke. "Do you think our store will burn, too?"

He tried not to dwell on the way she referred to it as their store. "Probably not, but I'm not taking any chances." Ethan secured Sadie in her car seat while Nicki stowed the bags and started the engine. He came around to her side of the car and leaned in the window. "Go straight to your mother's. Text me when you get there so I know you're safe."

"Aren't you coming with us? Ethan, you can't stay here."

"I'll be fine. Someone has to keep an eye on the store until the fire is under control. I'll keep you posted. Promise. Now go."

Ethan watched them disappear onto the back street, breathing a sigh of relief. He looked at the blaze now devouring the roof of the old building. He started back to the stairs, intending to watch from there until the blaze was put out.

As he approached the wooden stairs, a roar split the air. The sky was lit with a yellow glow and the air became harsh with the smell of smoke and burning materials. Ethan watched flames in the back windows licking their way up the other side of the roof. His mind began to close in, blurring the real world and drawing him back to a dusty market. His hands grew sweaty and started to shake. "No. Please, Lord. Not again."

Another boom tore reality from his grasp. He held his camera to his face, jogging backward, keeping the lens to his eye. He bumped into the Humvee, just as the market nearby exploded. A yell. A bright light. He ducked his head to avoid fallout from the missile explosion. He ran for cover, falling to his knees on the ground and covering his head. He heard someone shout and he crouched in the corner, praying. *The Lord is my shepherd.* Then everything went black.

"Hey, buddy. You okay?"

Ethan slowly opened his eyes. It was dark. The air was thick with the stench of water and burned wood. He looked up at a fireman, who was peering at him from beside the outside stairs.

"You okay? Did you get hit with debris? We have EMTs if you need help. Come on out of there."

Ethan glanced around, realizing he'd taken shelter beneath the landing of the old stairs. It hit him then. Flashback. He unfolded himself and came out to stand next to the fireman. A quick inventory revealed no damage. "I'm fine." His voice was weak and shaky.

"You sure?"

Ethan nodded. "Yeah. The explosion?"

"Took out the back wall on the second floor."

"How bad was the building damaged?"

"The building is a loss. Fortunately, the adjacent buildings weren't damaged. No one hurt. That's a good night."

After convincing the fireman he wasn't hurt, Ethan

looked at his phone and saw five texts from Nicki. He'd promised to keep her updated, but that was before the flashback had claimed him. How would he explain that to her? He'd thought he'd moved past that horror and found his footing again. Now his foundation was as unstable as the burned-out building.

Dragging his palms across his face, he sat on the wooden steps, fighting the waves of fear and discouragement swirling inside him like a hurricane. He needed to leave Dover and go back to Atlanta. If he stayed here, he might have another flashback. It would terrify Nicki.

He'd thought he was further along in his recovery. Yet he'd been yanked back again. He had no idea how long he'd been zoned out. He'd been a fool to let himself dream of a normal life.

He raked his hands along his scalp. It was time to go.

The smoke-filled air penetrated the inside of her car two blocks before she pulled into the alley behind the store. Nicki's heart beat double time, shortening her breath. Her mind swirled with a thousand terrifying scenarios of what might have happened to Ethan. Debi's advice after Jerry's shooting held new meaning now, too. Life was short. She needed to reach out for her future now. Debi had pointed out that it was difficult for some men to express themselves. Ethan had told her he'd lived his entire life from behind a camera. She should have realized it would be hard for him to admit his feelings. Especially after she'd kept talking about leaving. She wouldn't waste another moment. She'd tell Ethan she loved him, and she wanted him in her life, to be a father to Sadie, and she'd leave the outcome in the Lord's hands.

As she pulled up behind the store, she could see the

ugly black shell of the building where the insurance company had been located. She was thankful the fire had started while the office was closed.

But where was Ethan and why hadn't he called or answered her texts? Her headlights illuminated his parked car, so she knew he was here. She hurried up the stairs, coughing as the acrid air caught in her throat. Inside, she jogged to Ethan's door. Even here the air smelled of smoke.

"Ethan. Ethan, are you in there?" She waited, her breath stilling in her lungs. Why didn't he answer? Where was he? He had to be close by since his car was here. Had he tried to help with the fire and been injured?

"Ethan!" She pounded harder on the door.

It opened abruptly. Ethan stared back at her. "What are you doing here?"

She made a quick inventory. She saw no signs of injury, but when she looked into his eyes, her blood chilled. No warmth, no glint of affection, only a dull, detached look in the brown eyes. "Why didn't you call me and let me know you were all right? I texted you half a dozen times. What's wrong? Are you okay?" She reached out and touched his chest. He flinched as if she'd burned him.

"Ethan?"

He stepped aside to let her enter. What she saw stole the breath from her lungs. His duffel bag, the one she'd seen him with when he'd first moved into the apartment, was sitting on the kitchen table, stuffed with his clothes. A large black case sat on the floor nearby. His computer was closed, unplugged, the cord coiled on top.

"Why are you packing?"

Ethan kept his gaze averted, his hands on his hips.

"I'm going back to Atlanta. I've been offered a job taking pictures of returned veterans for a book. I think it's a good offer."

"You're leaving? Why? What happened?"

"Nothing."

"You're lying. Your eyes always give you away." She swiped unwelcome tears from the edges of her eyes. He stepped to her and pulled her close for a moment before leading her to the sofa.

Seated beside her, he took her hands in his. "Something happened tonight during the fire that makes it impossible for me to stay here."

She waited, trying to imagine anything that could have happened that would make him leave.

"I intended to come to your parents' house, but as I was watching the fire...I started to lose my grip. Then there was an explosion." He sucked in a deep breath. "I was back there, Nicki, in the middle of that marketplace, with the fire and the sounds and the horror."

He started to release her hand, but she gripped it tighter. She could feel him shaking. "Go on."

He stared at her hand, his thumb rubbing her skin. "I don't know how long I was out of it. The next thing I knew, a fireman was calling to me. I was huddled under the stairs like a scared kid." She squeezed his hand. "I can't stay here now."

"I don't understand. Why not?"

He stood. "Because I can't be responsible for what might happen to anyone around me when a flashback happens."

"What do you mean?"

"I lose myself. I think I'm back there and I have no awareness of what's going on around me. What if I had a flashback while I was watching Sadie and something happened to her? Or you needed me and I was lost in a mental battleground? It's dangerous."

He turned and faced her. The agony on his face tore at her heart. She didn't know how to help him. "Then you'll get help. We'll work together."

"My PTSD isn't going away, Nicki. It'll be with me forever. It can tear families apart. I'd thought I'd moved beyond the worst of it. Tonight proved I haven't."

He walked across the room before turning to face her, as if already breaking their bond. Nicki felt tears burning her eyes.

"Besides, you have a great job offer in Missouri. You are going to take it, aren't you?"

"I have to let them know today."

He nodded. "You'll be an asset to the company. They're lucky to get you."

Didn't he care? The raw emotion in his brown eyes said he cared very much. Now was the time. She had to tell him or regret it for the rest of her life. "I love you. I have for a while, but I was afraid to tell you. I'd made such a big deal of getting away from Dover, and I wasn't sure if you felt the same way. I thought you might, but you never said anything. But when you kissed me, I thought... Well, I didn't want you to leave without knowing how I felt."

He held her gaze a moment, his eyes warming with the light of love. "I've loved you from the moment I walked into this store. But it's because I love you that I need to go. You and Sadie mean everything to me."

"Then stay with us. Sadie and I need you."

Sadie and I need you. Nicki's parting words still reverberated in Ethan's mind. He'd led her to the door last night and practically shoved her out. He was doing the right thing for her and Sadie. She just didn't know it yet.

He glanced at the clock on the kitchen wall. Nicki would be at church soon. By the time the service ended, he'd be gone. He wasn't sure why he hadn't left last night. After Nicki had gone, he'd been too upset to think straight. He'd hoped a good night's sleep would help. It hadn't. He'd underestimated how hard it would be to walk away. Why had the Lord let him come here and fall in love and find a family, only to remind him he wasn't qualified for either role?

He'd called Paul last night, but even talking to him hadn't helped. Paul had accused him of being afraid for himself. That wasn't true. It was the first time Paul hadn't understood. That realization had hurt nearly as much as having to leave Nicki.

Ethan rested his palm against the window frame, staring out at the steeple. This would be the last time he'd see the inspiring sight. The thought stung like alcohol on an open wound. Rubbing his forehead, he turned away. His eyes burned from lack of sleep; every muscle in his body protested the fierce tension he'd been under since Nicki had confessed her love for him.

Before the fire, he would have soared on wings knowing his love was returned. But now, after last night, he had to turn her away. The flashback had stripped away all the progress he'd made. Nicki and Sadie had shown him how to live in the moment, how to embrace his emotions. He'd believed he'd finally found a place to belong. He liked being part of a community, the feelings of permanence and roots. He'd even started to believe that with Nicki's help he could learn to be a good father to Sadie. But now he had new fears to confront.

The flashback would always be lying in wait to possess him, and it could destroy his life and Nicki's, too.

His duffel bag was sitting open on the table. All he had left to pack were a few personal items. Mainly his Bible and a picture of Nicki and Sadie that he'd framed and kept in the bedroom. The first thing he saw when he woke up and the last thing he saw before falling asleep.

A knock on the door caught him by surprise. Nicki hadn't come back to the apartment last night. He'd assumed she'd stayed at her parents'. Had she come back to try to change his mind? He didn't think he could stand seeing her again. His heart would be blasted to smithereens.

He moved to the door and pulled it open, bracing himself to see Nicki. But it was her father who stood there.

"Mr. Latimer."

"May I come in?"

"Yes, of course. Is anything wrong with Nicki or Sadie?"

Latimer held his gaze. "In a way. My daughter is very upset, and I understand you're to blame for that."

Ethan dragged his hand across the back of his neck. "I'm sorry. I never wanted to hurt her."

Latimer moved the jacket lying on the sofa aside and sat down, crossing his legs, his posture indicating he wasn't leaving until he'd said his piece.

Ethan pulled a kitchen chair up, turned it around and straddled it, facing Nicki's father square on. Nothing was going to change his mind.

"She tells me you suffered a relapse last night during the fire."

A rush of heat rose up the back of his neck. He'd never intended to share his disorder with her father.

He saw now that he should have. "Yes. Which is why it's best that I leave."

"Is that the only reason?"

"Yes."

"You should know that my daughter tells me everything. I know that you believe your childhood makes you incapable of being a good husband and father."

Ethan might as well have stood before a firing squad. He swallowed the lump in his throat. "That's true. I have nothing to draw from."

"That makes you exactly like every other father on the planet. We all have to learn as we go."

"I don't want to make any mistakes. They mean too much to me."

"If that's true, then everything you need to know about being a good father is right there in that book."

Ethan didn't have to look to know Latimer was referring to the Bible lying beside his duffel.

"But I have a feeling that your decision to leave is based more on your own fears than your true feelings."

He had no answer for him. That was what scared him. The unknown.

"My daughter is a strong-willed, determined woman. And when she gives her heart, it's forever. She made a terrible mistake before, but I don't think she's made one this time. I think she's given her heart to someone who can make her happy and still allow her the independence she needs." Latimer stood. "And from what I've seen over the last weeks, you need her and my granddaughter in your life, too."

Ethan followed him to the door. "I love them both, Mr. Latimer. More than anything."

"Then give them the chance to love you back. Don't throw away my girls because of something that might not ever happen." He rested a comforting hand on Ethan's shoulder. "There's a place for you in our family. Whatever troubles you bring with you, we'll be there to help."

He opened the door then turned back. "Today is Mother's Day. Nicki's first." He held Ethan's gaze a long moment. Then left.

Ethan shut the door, his thoughts more confused than ever. If he believed Nicki's father, then walking away from her would be the worst mistake he could make. He knew that, but that didn't erase his deep concern about his flashbacks. Latimer's words had echoed Paul's. Was he more fearful of having a flashback or of taking on the responsibility of becoming a husband and father?

His gaze came to rest on his worn Bible. Taking a seat at the table, he shoved aside the duffel bag and opened the book, thinking about the fathers in scripture and the Father in Heaven. One particular father came to mind: Joseph. He must have felt equally inadequate to become a father. There'd been no guidebook for raising the Son of God. How had he done it? How had he found the courage?

He knew the answer. Faith. Trust. The Lord had brought Ethan through so much. Why did he doubt that He could bring him through the experience of fatherhood? He picked up the picture of Nicki and Sadie. His life would be meaningless and empty without them. Today was Mother's Day. Nicki's first. More than anything, he wanted to celebrate it with her. Maybe it was time to stop hiding behind his fears and step out in faith.

Church was already letting out at Peace Community when Ethan approached the front sidewalk. He'd forgotten that their service was earlier than Hope Chapel's. He searched the members as they emerged, looking for Nicki. Had she even come today? Maybe she had been too upset. He should have asked her dad this morning when he'd come by.

Ethan spotted Nicki's parents as they exited the front door. Mr. Latimer saw him, smiled and pointed toward the side of the church. Ethan nodded and walked around to the side. He saw Nicki emerge carrying Sadie. They made a beautiful sight. The mother and child. When he saw them together now, he never thought about the others. The Lord had helped him heal from that incident by giving him a new image to overlay it.

He hurried forward. She saw him and stopped. Her blue eyes were clouded with sadness. She raised her chin as if defying him to hurt her anymore.

"Did you come to say goodbye?"

"No. I came to tell you happy Mother's Day. I didn't want to miss your first one." The disappointment in her blue eyes wounded him. He was making a mess of this. "Is there someplace we can talk?"

She held his gaze a moment, then gestured toward the back of the church. He followed her into a walled garden tucked into a small grove of trees behind the sanctuary. Nicki sat on a wooden bench, settling the baby in her lap. Ethan held his breath as he took a seat beside them. Slowly he took her hand. "Nicki, I love you. I realized that losing you and Sadie would be more traumatic than the explosion or the picture or anything I've ever experienced. I'd never recover. I want to share the rest of my life with you. If that means moving to Branson or Boston, it doesn't matter." He held his breath, waiting for her response.

"Are you sure?"

"Yes. I've never been more sure of anything in my life."

"Ethan, I didn't take the job in Branson. I want Sadie

to grow up in Dover and to know her grandparents. I realized it would be cruel to take her away from them, and I've discovered I can't raise her by myself. I could, but I want her to have family. And a father."

Ethan's heart threatened to burst from his chest. He pulled her close, wrapping his arms around her and baby Sadie. The kiss he gave her promised a future full of happiness.

"What about the photo job in Atlanta?"

"I can still do it. It might mean a few weeks of travel here and there, but—" he reached out and touched her cheek "—I know my independent wife will be able to handle things while I'm gone."

A beautiful, loving smile lit Nicki's face. "I'm not so independent that I don't know I need you in my life. Forever."

Ethan leaned toward her, placing a tender kiss on her lips. Sadie squealed and waved her hands. "Does that mean she likes the idea?"

"Of course. She loves you." Nicki handed the baby to Ethan. "I have something for you. I was going to give it to you before, but then I heard about the settlement, and then the fire, and, well…this is the perfect time." She pulled a small envelope from her bag, slipped something out and handed it to him.

Ethan took the small card and turned it over. It was a photograph of the three of them. He was holding Sadie, and Nicki was smiling up at him. "When did you take this?"

"I had my dad take it last Sunday when we were at the house. It's for your wallet."

Ethan's throat tightened with gratitude. "It's perfect. Thank you."

"I think we make a good-looking family, don't you?"

"I think we're picture perfect." He stood, pulling Nicki up and wrapping the three of them in his embrace. The bond he'd felt the first time he'd held Sadie had become a reality. They were a family at last.

* * * * *

Dear Reader,

I don't remember when I first got the idea for this book. I suspect it was from an article I read someplace, but once the idea took hold I couldn't let it go. Perhaps it was because Ethan wasn't the type of hero we usually associate with PTSD. A conflict photographer who captures one too many horrific images of war, rather than a soldier in the military.

Finding the perfect heroine for him took some work, but I think Nicki and baby Sadie were the answer. Both Ethan and Nicki endured traumatic events that left them questioning who they were and forced them to turn their lives in new directions. The Lord placed them in each other's paths to help them heal and start a new life together as a family.

I hope you enjoy this trip to Dover, Mississippi. There are more stories from the small town coming up. Please come back and visit.

You can contact me through Love Inspired Books or at lorrainebeatty.com.

Lorraine

Questions for Discussion

1. Nicki felt her mother didn't approve of anything she did. How often do you seek self-worth in what other people think?

2. Ethan believes that his time in the foster-care system disqualified him from being a good husband and father. What does the Lord tell us about overcoming our past?

3. Nicki has the burden of saving her family business. Have you ever been in the position of having to carry the load for others? How did you feel?

4. Traumatic events in our lives can force us to rethink who we are. Have you had an event in your life that made you reevaluate yourself and your future? Share ways that you found to help you.

5. Nicki had a plan for her future and nothing was going to get in her way. How did her stubbornness complicate her life? Have you ever made a decision and refused to change it?

6. Ethan used his camera as a shield to protect his emotions. How can avoiding our feelings lead to problems? What are some healthy ways to deal with our emotions?

7. Do you think Ethan had good cause to doubt his ability to be a good father? Why or why not?

8. Nicki's greatest strength, her independent streak, was also her greatest weakness. Do you agree or disagree?

9. Talking about our fears and pains is difficult but helpful. Have you found this to be true? Share your experience with others.

10. Both Nicki and Ethan have a strong faith and proof that the Lord had carried them through difficult times, yet both failed to trust Him with certain heart matters. Why do you think they did that?

11. Ethan benefited from a friend's help and tried to reach out to help another. How can going through a difficult event enable you to help others?

12. Both Ethan and Nicki were reluctant to express their feelings to one another. Do you think they should have spoken up sooner? Why or why not?

COMING NEXT MONTH FROM
Love Inspired®

Available November 18, 2014

HER MONTANA CHRISTMAS
Big Sky Centennial • by Arlene James

When town historian Robin Frazier agrees to help pastor Ethan Johnson decorate the church for a centennial Christmas celebration, she never expects to fall for him. Will revealing her secret ruin everything?

A RANCHER FOR CHRISTMAS
Martin's Crossing • by Brenda Minton

Breezy Hernandez is surprised to learn she's sharing custody of her twin nieces with rancher Jake Martin. Can she convince the handsome cowboy she's mom—and wife—material?

AN AMISH CHRISTMAS JOURNEY
Brides of Amish Country • by Patricia Davids

Toby Yoder's journey to bring his sister home for Christmas is thwarted when a blizzard strands them at Greta Barkman's home. What starts out as a mission of kindness soon becomes a journey of the heart.

YULETIDE BABY
Cowboy Country • by Deb Kastner

Cowboy pastor Shawn O'Riley never expected to get a baby for Christmas. Asking experienced foster mom Heather Lewis for help with the infant left in his church's nativity set might just give him the greatest gift of all—family.

HER HOLIDAY FAMILY
Kirkwood Lake • by Ruth Logan Herne

Former army captain Max Campbell is back in town to help his ailing dad. Can he prove to old love Tina Martinelli that's he's sticking around, not just for the holidays, but for forever?

SUGAR PLUM SEASON
Barrett's Mill • by Mia Ross

Amy Morgan hires Jason Barrett to build sets for her dance school's holiday performance. Soon she'll have to choose between her ballerina dreams and building a future with the charming lumberjack.

LOOK FOR THESE AND OTHER LOVE INSPIRED BOOKS WHEREVER BOOKS ARE SOLD, INCLUDING MOST BOOKSTORES, SUPERMARKETS, DISCOUNT STORES AND DRUGSTORES.

LICNM1114

REQUEST YOUR FREE BOOKS!

2 FREE INSPIRATIONAL NOVELS
PLUS 2
FREE
MYSTERY GIFTS

Love Inspired®

YES! Please send me 2 FREE Love Inspired® novels and my 2 FREE mystery gifts (gifts are worth about $10). After receiving them, if I don't wish to receive any more books, I can return the shipping statement marked "cancel." If I don't cancel, I will receive 6 brand-new novels every month and be billed just $4.74 per book in the U.S. or $5.24 per book in Canada. That's a saving of at least 21% off the cover price. It's quite a bargain! Shipping and handling is just 50¢ per book in the U.S. and 75¢ per book in Canada.* I understand that accepting the 2 free books and gifts places me under no obligation to buy anything. I can always return a shipment and cancel at any time. Even if I never buy another book, the two free books and gifts are mine to keep forever.

105/305 IDN F47Y

Name _____ (PLEASE PRINT)

Address _____ Apt. #

City _____ State/Prov. _____ Zip/Postal Code

Signature (if under 18, a parent or guardian must sign)

Mail to the Harlequin® Reader Service:
IN U.S.A.: P.O. Box 1867, Buffalo, NY 14240-1867
IN CANADA: P.O. Box 609, Fort Erie, Ontario L2A 5X3

**Are you a subscriber to Love Inspired books
and want to receive the larger-print edition?
Call 1-800-873-8635 or visit www.ReaderService.com.**

* Terms and prices subject to change without notice. Prices do not include applicable taxes. Sales tax applicable in N.Y. Canadian residents will be charged applicable taxes. Offer not valid in Quebec. This offer is limited to one order per household. Not valid for current subscribers to Love Inspired books. All orders subject to credit approval. Credit or debit balances in a customer's account(s) may be offset by any other outstanding balance owed by or to the customer. Please allow 4 to 6 weeks for delivery. Offer available while quantities last.

Your Privacy—The Harlequin® Reader Service is committed to protecting your privacy. Our Privacy Policy is available online at www.ReaderService.com or upon request from the Harlequin Reader Service.

We make a portion of our mailing list available to reputable third parties that offer products we believe may interest you. If you prefer that we not exchange your name with third parties, or if you wish to clarify or modify your communication preferences, please visit us at www.ReaderService.com/consumerschoice or write to us at Harlequin Reader Service Preference Service, P.O. Box 9062, Buffalo, NY 14269. Include your complete name and address.

LI13R

SPECIAL EXCERPT FROM

Love Inspired

Don't miss the conclusion of the
***BIG SKY CENTENNIAL** miniseries!*
Here's a sneak peek at HER MONTANA CHRISTMAS
by Arlene James:

"Robin," Ethan said, just before his face appeared in the church belfry's open trapdoor, "come on up. It's perfectly safe."

He reached down a gloved hand as she put a foot on the bottom rung of the wrought-iron ladder.

"How does this thing work?"

"It's very simple. There's a tall pole with a hook on one end. I used it to slide open the trap and then pull down the ladder. When I'm done, I'll use it to push the ladder back up and lift it over the locking mechanism, then slide the trap closed."

"I see."

"Oh, you haven't seen anything yet," he told her, grasping her hand and all but lifting her up the last few rungs to stand next to him on a narrow metal platform. In their bulky coats, they had to stand pressed shoulder to shoulder. "Take a look at this." He swung his arm wide, encompassing the town, the valley beyond and the snow-capped mountains surrounding it all.

"Wow."

"Exactly," he said. "There's a part of Psalms 98 that says, 'Let the rivers clap their hands, let the mountains sing together for joy…' Seeing the view like this, you can almost feel it, can't you? The rivers and mountains praising their Creator."

"I never thought of rivers and mountains praising God," she admitted.

"Scripture speaks many times of nature praising God and testifying to His wonders."

"I can see why," she said reverently.

"So can I," he told her, smiling down at her with those warm brown eyes.

Her breath caught in her throat. But surely she was reading too much into that look. That wasn't appreciation she saw in his gaze. That was just her loneliness seeking connection. Wasn't it? Though she had never felt this sudden, electrical link before, as if something vital and masculine in him reached out and touched something fundamental and feminine in her. She had to be mistaken.

He was a man of God, after all.

Even if she couldn't help thinking of him as just a man.

Will Robin and Ethan find love for Christmas, or will her secrets stand in their way? Find out in HER MONTANA CHRISTMAS by Arlene James, available December 2014 wherever Love Inspired® books and ebooks are sold.

Copyright © 2014 by Deborah A. Rather

LIEXP1114